SURPRISE ATTACK

The aircar bucked through wicked thermals as we raced for the Academy, ever mindful of the destruction clearly visible in the rearview-screen. The Dalgiri shuttle was a tiny black speck moving toward the invisible volume of space which was the portal between this time-line and the next.

I stepped up the magnification until the shuttle was a black circle against the brilliant blue sky. Suddenly a dozen more specks materialized in the open sky around it. We were dead. Thirteen Dalgiri shuttles carried enough firepower to make Salfa Prime uninhabitable for the rest of eternity.

I had time to gulp once more before there was a brilliant flash behind us, more brilliant than the others by an order of magnitude. My head and shoulders were suddenly aflame where they projected above the curve of the aircar body.

I opened my mouth to yell as the aircar's nose burrowed into the wet and icy cold . . .

A Greater Infinity

by Michael McCollum

A Del Rey Book

BALLANTINE BOOKS • NEW YORK

A Del Rey Book
Published by Ballantine Books

Copyright © 1979, 1980, 1981, 1982 by Michael McCollum

A GREATER INFINITY was previously published in three
parts in *Analog* magazine: July 1979; November 1980; and
July 1981.

Library of Congress Catalog Card Number: 81-68648

ISBN 0-345-30167-6

Manufactured in the United States of America

First Edition: February 1982

Cover art by David B. Mattingly

TO CATHERINE
for letting me type
all those evenings

CHAPTER 1

Dɪᴅ you ever dream of doing great things with your life? You know, wish you had discovered penicillin, or a lost continent, or been a great general? Hal Benson is like that. Hal is my landlord and a good friend. But he lets his enthusiasms get the best of him. Not that his dreams are any of the things I just mentioned. Hal's dreams are more in keeping with the times. And unlike most people, he acts to bring them to pass. It makes him a bit strange. In fact, Hal is something of a crackpot.

Chief among his interests is his abiding faith in life on other planets. True, he's also the local guru of the science-fiction fan club and something called the Society for Creative Anachronism, but his main interest is the UFO Spotters Club, of which he is founder and president. The three groups consist of an amorphous clique of lovers of the unknown who seem to travel through life in their own private worlds, unaffected by the things the rest of humanity considers important.

And that brings me in a roundabout way to my story. It has nothing to do with Hal Benson, although he did act as the catalyst so I thought I ought to mention him.

It was midwinter, one of those crystal-clear nights when a freezing wind whips in off the desert from the east and the Moon bathes everything in a bright, pearly glow. Hal was off to a science-fiction convention back East and the UFO Spotters were using our place—a dilapidated rooming house in the old section of Tempe near the university —for their monthly meeting. Since I was the only resident in residence (the others having taken off for parts unknown, it being semester break), I was assigned the job of keeping them from tearing up the place and making sure the cops had no probable cause for a drug bust.

They came drifting in about eight, and by the time the formal meeting had started, fifty-odd people were scattered in nooks and crannies around the old house. And I mean fifty *odd* people! In Hal's absence, Weasel Martin took over the meeting. Weasel is a short, bearded graduate student whose most prominent feature is his nervous tic. He banged on a table with a wooden spoon to get attention, then called the meeting to order.

I was in the kitchen dishing out taco chips and bean dip. Jane Dugway was helping me, as well as pulling the pop tops from the half-case of Coors. Somehow the cans disappeared into the other room as fast as she opened them.

I had first met Jane at school. Even though I was majoring in engineering, the university was determined that I get a well-rounded education. So in order to complete my eight hours of social sciences required to graduate, I took a course in anthropology. Jane was a graduate student in anthro and my discussion-group leader for one semester. She wasn't one of those lucky women blessed with the gift of beauty. Her hair had terminal frizzies, and Coke-bottle glasses did nothing to improve her profile. But the mind behind her mannish face was as sharp as a razor blade.

We carried the taco chips and bean dip into the living room just as Weasel Martin called for old business. PeeJay Schwarz got to his feet and began an excited narrative about an Alabama farmer who claimed to have been to the Moon on a flying saucer. Weasel ruled him out of order. PeeJay's an overweight teenager with a bad skin condition and the personality of a bantam cock, so Weasel's censure didn't bother him at all. He just got red in the face and talked louder.

Weasel took a couple of menacing steps toward PeeJay, his hands clenched into two white-knuckled fists, and his tic going a mile a minute. Gordon Trackmann, a grandfatherly type with a crewcut, stepped between them and got PeeJay cooled down with a promise that he could speak first when the agenda turned to new business.

After that things settled down considerably. It might as

well have been a meeting of the League of Women Voters, with everything being run in strict adherence to Robert's Rules of Order. I was fast losing interest when Joel Peterson decided to launch the evening's debate. Joel is a prissy sociology major who wears bow ties with his blue denim shirts and dirty Levi's. He revels in being the club skeptic and is especially skilled in sparking controversy.

"I don't believe in UFOs," he declared loudly. "Not as interstellar visitors, anyway."

There was a murmured undercurrent in the crowd—the sort of thing that happens in the movies just before the lynching—and Weasel Martin prepared to smite the unbeliever with lightning.

"Then you're dumber than you look," he said to Joel. A scattering of applause sounded and someone muttered, "That must be pretty dumb considering his looks."

I had to give Joel credit. He stood his ground. "What makes you think UFOs aren't just a mammoth hoax? Have *you* ever seen one?" It was a good attack. Although several members claimed to have spotted UFOs, everyone knew that Weasel Martin never had, and that he considered it a personal affront.

The wrangling went on for another half-hour before Weasel got fed up. "Okay, smart ass! If they aren't visitors from other stars, what are they? And don't tell me swamp gas!"

There was a pause, and a smug look spread across Joel's face. His trap had been set, baited, and sprung. "They're time travelers from the future or from a parallel universe," he said in triumph.

This was greeted by a chorus of Bronx cheers, boos, and catcalls. Weasel was about to launch his counterattack when Sam Grohs pushed open the kitchen door and diverted everyone's attention.

"Hey, what happened to the beer?"

"Gone," I said.

"Gone? Hey, man, I'm dying of thirst."

Then the chorus began—"BEER RUN, BEER RUN. WE WANT A BEER RUN!"

Weasel took time out from the debate to look around. He found a discarded cowboy hat and passed it to the assembled congregation. "Okay, you turkeys. Ante up for a beer run."

While the hat made the rounds, Joel gave us all the once-over. "Who's going to make this run?"

"Duncan MacElroy," someone in back piped up. "He's not doing anything."

The chant began again. "DUNCAN, DUNCAN, DUNCAN!"

I didn't join the chanting. I'm Duncan and I didn't want to go out into the cold.

"How about it, MacElroy?" Weasel asked. "Want to make a beer run?"

I shrugged. "Why not? But I can't carry it all by myself."

"I'll go."

I turned around to see Jane Dugway get to her feet. I might have predicted it would be her. Jane is one of the few people in the club who ever volunteer for anything.

"Okay, Jane. Wait a sec while I get my coat."

Jane waited for me on the sidewalk out front. She was bundled up in a fur coat with her black leather bag over one shoulder.

"Got the money?" I asked.

She nodded. "Shall we drive?"

I looked around. I could barely see my Jag through the cluster of cars that slopped over from the driveway onto the front lawn.

"I'm parked in," I said.

"Me too. I guess we walk."

"Okay," I said. "It's only two blocks."

We set out at a leisurely pace up Oak toward the red and white sign of our local convenience market. The rest of the houses on the street were dark because of midsemester break. Every couple of blocks a mercury vapor lamp illuminated a streetcorner. But the long spaces between were dark patches of flickering moonlight and shadow. The sidewalk was a white lane barred with the shadows of bare tree limbs, broken in dozens of spots where clumps of winter grass pushed up through cracks left by sixty years of summer heat and winter cold.

The liquor coolers of the market were sparse hunting. We finally ended up with half a dozen six-packs of four different kinds of beer. We loaded them into bags and started for home.

The conversation drifted to anthropology. I walked in front of Jane, feeling my way over the tilted, broken slabs of sidewalk, discussing a pet theory I'd developed about the affinity of modern Americans for vicarious enjoyment via the boob tube. Suddenly I felt a hard shoulder in the small of my back and was flying into a hedge of Texas sage. I landed on my belly as the beer crashed to the ground with a metallic clatter. Two of the cans burst open, spraying me with a cold shower of carbonated hops.

I spit out a mouthful of dirt and grass, and turned over. It was dark in the shadow of the hedge, but I could make out Jane, flat on her stomach, peering down and across the street at something.

"What was that for?" I asked.

"Quiet," she hissed.

"What the hell is going on here?" I asked, sitting up and brushing the sticky beer from my jacket. I wrinkled my nose at the smell.

She reached up with one arm and pulled me down again. She was surprisingly strong and I could feel the bruises on my upper arm where she had grabbed me.

"If you value your life, stay down!"

I opened my mouth to reply, then shut it again. I had just caught sight of the gun.

Except it wasn't a gun. Even with only scattered patches of moonlight to see by, that much was obvious. The thing in her hand was a weapon of some kind. It had a handle, a trigger, and a trigger guard. But the barrel was a long thin glass pipe that glowed with a faint blue fluorescence. My mind sorted through its dusty files and came up with a name for that glow. Cherenkov radiation! It was the glow of a nuclear reactor under two dozen feet of water.

"What's going on?" I asked.

"Over there," she said, gesturing toward a large hedge halfway down the block on the other side. "At the base of the oleanders, about twenty feet from the end."

I strained my eyes, conscious of how the cold wind bit into me where the beer had soaked into my clothes. The spot she described was fairly well lighted by the corner street lamp. "I don't see anything."

"Look closely at the area that seems to be fading out of focus."

I squinted. I wasn't sure, but I thought I saw what she referred to. Some trick of light and shadow caused a small section of bushes to advance and recede while I watched. It was like watching something under running water.

"I see it," I said.

"That's a Dalgiri aversion field. One of them is watching your house."

"What's a Dalgiri?" I asked, thinking I was being set up for a joke. You know: "What's a Greek urn? Oh, about two dollars an hour."

"A Near Man and my mortal enemy," she said, glancing up and down the street. The lenses of her glasses caught the light from the street lamp, causing them to flash with blue-white fire as she moved her head. Somehow she didn't look the type to have enemies. "He will try to kill me if he can. You too, I'm afraid, if he sees us together."

"What the hell is going on here, Jane?"

"*Shh.*" She placed a finger to her lips. "I'll neutralize him. You stay put."

Without waiting for an answer, she crawled into the black, leaving me to listen to the rustle of the wind through the bare limbs of the trees. A block away I could hear the swish of tires on pavement.

I lay still for nearly five minutes, feeling more foolish by the second. Joel Peterson had put her up to this, I decided. It was just his kind of joke. The whole UFO Spotters Club was probably camped in one of the darkened upstairs bedrooms having a good laugh at me. I felt a flush rise in my cheeks. I got to my hands and knees and peered over the Texas sage.

A bolt of lightning flashed before my eyes.

No thunderclap answered, no sound at all. But the searing light cut into my eyes like a knife, followed quickly by a sudden wave of heat. I dropped to my stomach once more, whimpering. The night returned to normal. Darkness closed in again except for the afterimage of the flash that continued to dance before my eyes. And besides the odor of stale beer, another stink penetrated my nostrils—the strong smell of ozone.

Nothing happened for two minutes and I risked raising my head once more. The white splotches were still carved into my retinas, but my vision was clear enough for me to see Jane make a crouching run across the street to where the oleanders reached the sidewalk on the other side. She disappeared into the dark. I waited one more minute, then scrambled to my feet and raced after her.

I found her kneeling over the body of a man. He'd been no beauty in life, and his looks hadn't improved in death. He stared unseeing at the Moon, a gaping hole burned in his chest. The wound smelled of seared flesh. I gagged twice, trying to keep the beer and taco chips down.

"My God, Jane! What have you done?"

She looked over her shoulder at me. "I thought I told you to stay where you were?"

"You killed him!"

"He would have killed me."

"With what? For all you know he was just some poor Peeping Tom."

She felt around in the bushes where the dead man's hand disappeared into the shadows, and came up with a gun similar to hers. It too had an oddly shining glass barrel.

"What's going on here?"

"No time, Duncan." She turned to look directly into my eyes. "I need your help. Where there's one Dalgir, there will be others. Can I count on you?"

"Sorry, but when it comes to murder, I draw the line. See you around!" I backed out of the hedge hastily, turning to run.

"Wait!"

I felt a prickling sensation run up my spine. I'd almost forgotten the gun she held.

"For what?" I asked, turning back to her.

"Hear me out. Then if you want to leave, go ahead."

"Okay, start talking."

"Well, firstly—this is a Dalgir, a Near Man."

"Okay, you've already told me that. Now what exactly is a Dalgir?"

"You would call him a Neanderthal. One of a race that

died out fifty thousand years ago on this timeline. On others, however, they survived and prospered. It is such a line that I and my people war against."

I looked at the corpse. Damned if he didn't look like the Neanderthal exhibits in the museums. Jutting bony eye ridges, sloping forehead, slouching posture as he lay in death. But the Neanderthalers in the museums hadn't worn hunting clothes straight out of the Sears Roebuck catalog. And they hadn't carried glass-barreled pistols that emitted Cherenkov radiation.

"Timeline?"

"An alternate universe with its own history, culture, and peoples. Joel Peterson was speculating on the concept only half an hour ago."

"I hope you think up a better story than that before the police arrive." I turned once more to leave.

"If I'm not from a parallel universe, how do you explain these?" She gestured to the two guns. Her voice carried a hint of humor.

She had me there. I'd attended a couple of lectures on laser weapons. Every expert agreed that a laser pistol was a theoretical impossibility. Except a man lay dead at my feet with a hole burned in his chest by just such a weapon.

"Okay," I said. "Let's suppose you are telling the truth. What do you want me to do about it?"

"This Dalgir was waiting to ambush me. They aren't even supposed to know about this timeline. The encounter must be reported."

"So report," I said. "But take this body with you when you go."

"I need you, Duncan. You have to help me dispose of the body. It would never do to have it discovered by the police."

I chewed my lip. I'd never even been late paying a parking ticket. And here I was being asked to help cover up a cold-blooded murder!

So why did I choose to help her? I'm not sure, even now. It certainly wasn't because she was beautiful. Maybe down deep, I believed her story.

"Okay," I said, regretting the decision even as I made it. "What do you want me to do?"

"We need to dump the body where it won't be found for eight hours or so."

I lifted my right arm and pointed west. "A weed-filled ditch parallels the Southern Pacific tracks half a block over."

"It'll have to do. Grab his arms. I'll take the legs."

"No."

"What?" she asked, perplexed.

"No. Not until you hand over that firepower."

Indecision flashed across her face.

"Look, Jane, you are going to have to trust me. You haven't any choice."

"You'll see me safely away?"

I nodded. "I don't know why I believe such an obviously ridiculous story—" She opened her mouth to say something. I held up my hand and she shut it with a snap. "—I know, you've got a Buck Rogers ray gun. Maybe that's enough, maybe not. In either event, hand both of them over or I take a walk."

She bit her lower lip, but held out her hand with the two lasers. I took them. They were warm to the touch.

"These emit anything that might disagree with my gonads?"

She shook her head. "Both beamers are well shielded."

I slipped the guns into my belt in back, under my jacket. "Fine, let's get rid of Mr. America."

The Neanderthal was heavier than he looked. He was barely five feet tall, but chunky. We half-carried half-dragged him through deserted backyards and trash-strewn alleys. When we finally lowered his body at the edge of the ditch, I stood up and puffed from exertion.

"Strip him!" Jane said, working to loosen the leather belt he wore. A dozen or so pouches protruded from the belt and she began to sort through them.

"What have you got there?" I whispered as I worked to peel his pants off.

"Equipment kit," she whispered back. She pulled each strange mechanism out of its pouch, examined it, then replaced it. About the time I had managed to remove the Dalgir's shirt, she seemed to find what she was looking for. It looked like a tear-gas pen.

"Okay," I said as I stripped the last of the clothing off the body. "What now?"

The Dalgir lay obscenely exposed in the moonlight, but not because he was naked. It had more to do with the hole in his chest.

"Roll him face down into the ditch and then step back." Jane pulled on gloves from her purse then held the tear-gas pen gingerly in her gloved hand.

"What's in that thing?"

"A specially mutated bacteria. Get any of it on you and you'll be dead of what appears to be leprosy in a matter of hours."

That was enough warning for me. I backpedaled a good fifty feet, carrying the bundle of clothing with me. She bent over the body and did something with the pen. What she did made a certain amount of sense . . . in a gross way.

How does one solve the problem of introducing a strain of man-eating germs into a corpse? You can't very well ask the victim to swallow a pill. But we sometimes forget that the mouth is only one of two openings into the alimentary canal. Jane used the other.

She quickly rejoined me, carefully pulled off the gloves, and buried them in the center of the clothing, which she tied in a bundle. She leaned down and stuffed the bundle into an old tire.

"Let's go back for the beer. The others will be getting worried." As she turned to leave, the light caught her face. Droplets of perspiration glistened on her forehead in spite of the chill wind that blew.

"What about? . . ." I thrust my thumb over my shoulder toward the irrigation ditch.

"In eight hours there will be no trace of our departed Dalgir. Now we have to report."

"How?" I asked. "I'm afraid my subspace radio is broken at the moment."

She laughed, a high nervous giggle. Reaction was setting in. "Then we'll just have to rely on Ma Bell. We'll use the phone in the rooming house."

The debate was still going hot and heavy. I lugged the beer into the kitchen while Jane went to the telephone in the hall. She carried it to the length of its cord into the bathroom and shut and locked the door. I stationed myself outside on guard duty. With my ear half pressed against the wall I could barely make out her side of the conversation. Not that it did me a lot of good. She spoke quickly in a language that was more than a little reminiscent of French. After a few minutes in which she did most of the talking—to judge by the short silences—she said good-bye in English and hung up.

I was waiting for her when she unlocked the door and stepped into the hall. "Well?"

"They're sending a shuttle to pick me up. It will arrive tomorrow after sundown."

"Where?"

"The Mogollon Rim, north of Payson."

"I know the area. One of my uncles has a cabin outside Christopher Creek at the base of the Rim."

"Then you'll take me there? I don't dare use my car. They may have put a tracer on it."

"You're out of luck. The whole north country is knee-deep in snow this time of year. My Jag was never designed to play snowmobile. We'll have to find a jeep."

Tony Minetti chose that time to head for the bathroom. He heard the last of our conversation.

"Jeep?" he asked. It was then that I remembered Tony had a relic of the Second World War that he kept parked in front of his apartment building six blocks away.

"Yeah," I said. "I promised Jane I would drive her up to Payson tonight. She just remembered that her Aunt Agatha was expecting her for the holidays. How about it, Tony? Can we borrow your jeep?"

"I don't know, man. You're talking about my pride and joy." He wrinkled his nose. "Boy, you smell like a brewery, Dunc!"

"Spilled some beer on myself." I took a deep breath and made the ultimate sacrifice. "I'll let you borrow my XKE." Tony had cast a lecherous eye on my car for as long as I'd known him.

"It's a deal, man!"

We exchanged keys with me wondering if I was making the mistake of my life. Jane and I went to my bedroom and dug in the closet for some warm clothes.

When we were properly outfitted—Jane with my blue B-9 parka over her coat and me in a heavy leather jacket and snow boots—we slipped out the back. Joel Peterson was screaming something about parallel universes while the crowd around him booed.

As I stepped out into the cold dark on the back porch, I couldn't help smiling.

CHAPTER 2

ARIZONA—land of parched, overheated deserts and a dozen different kinds of poisonous insect, snake, and lizard. Where rain doesn't fall for six months at a time and the natives huddle in air-conditioned warrens for a quarter of the year, dashing outside only long enough to dodge from one cool hidey-hole to another. Right?

Half right. That's a pretty accurate picture of the southern desert. The northern part of the state, on the other hand, is blanketed with high mountains and lush forests. Driving down from Detroit on the Interstate, I had been amazed at the amount of climatic variation that could be found in a hundred-mile stretch. It made for interesting driving.

Except now I was driving like a madman into the high country in a forty-year-old jeep whose canvas top had never been meant to withstand a dozen years of desert sun. Two gaping holes allowed in a freezing slipstream of air to overpower the ancient heater. Jane and I were nearly blue with cold as the wan yellow headlight beams fell on the dilapidated log walls of my uncle's hunting cabin.

I pulled off the road into the high snowdrifts surrounding the cabin. The jeep's transfer case growled in protest as we slithered and bulled our way the last hundred feet. It almost sounded grateful as I turned the key, allowing the wheezing old engine finally to rest. I left the lights on to show the way to the front porch, with me breaking trail and Jane stumbling behind, shivering.

It was three A.M.

I got the door open and ushered her inside, before going back out to turn off the headlights. When I returned to the cabin, she had set up something that gave off a pearly white glow on the kitchen counter. I glanced at it and recognized one of the devices we'd removed from the Dalgir. I headed for the fireplace and began stacking wood against the blackened grate. Within five minutes cheerful tongues of flame were licking at the wood.

"Get over by the fire," I told her. "I'll go and start the generator."

My boots made soft crunching noises as I pushed through the virgin snow out back of the cabin. By the time I'd plowed a path to the shed—actually an old outhouse that had been expanded and converted for storage —I was panting from the high altitude and unaccustomed exertion. In spite of the cold, sweat beads rolled down my back. I took off my fur-lined jacket and hung it on a nail in the generator shack.

I checked the gas and oil in the old generator, using a flashlight I'd picked up in the cabin. Crossing my fingers, I pulled on the starter rope. For once the motor roared to life on the first try. I fiddled with the choke until the inevitable hiccups passed. Throwing the large knife switch on the cobwebbed wall, I listened for the sound of the generator coming on line. Its bearings had been deteriorating for the two years I'd been using the cabin, and when an electric load was applied, it would clatter softly as it turned.

When I got back to the cabin, the fire had taken some of the nip out of the air and the lights were burning brightly. I began to unlace my boots. It had been one *helluva* night and I was dead tired. Jane was puttering around in the bathroom, doing I had no idea what. With the water turned off for the winter to keep from bursting a pipe, the bathroom was one of the less functional rooms in the cabin.

I busied myself with the fire until I heard her soft steps behind me.

"Well, what do you think?" she asked.

I turned around. "What do I think about what—" I caught my breath.

She stood on the Navajo rug in front of the fire and posed like a model out of *Mademoiselle*. She had made dramatic changes in her looks. Her hair was neatly combed, no longer standing out at right angles to her head. Her Coke-bottle glasses were gone, revealing a sensitive pair of eyes that were now violet. They had been brown. She had done something to her face, too. What, I couldn't be sure. It was a bit rounder and softer than it had been.

She still wasn't beautiful, but she was far from ugly. In fact, she was quite pleasant-looking. As I stood speechless and checked out the changes, I noticed that her figure seemed to have improved as well.

"Like it?" she asked, pirouetting for me.

"What happened?"

"How do they say it on television?—my cover is blown so there is no need to continue the masquerade."

Her comment brought me back to reality, a place I hadn't been in a number of hours. "Which reminds me. Tell me about parallel universes."

She bit her lower lip and looked worried. "I suppose I do owe you an explanation, Duncan." She sat cross-legged on the couch, patting the cushion next to her. I sat down beside her and noticed her perfume for the first time.

My heart began to beat faster. "You can begin anytime," I said, more to change the subject of my thoughts than anything else.

She looked down at the floor. "I really shouldn't. It's against regulations to discuss Paratime with the natives."

"We're both a little bit pregnant in that department, aren't we?"

"A little bit? . . ." She looked puzzled for an instant, then she laughed. "I see what you mean. After last night, the regulations don't make very much sense, do they?"

"No, they don't."

"I won't bore you with the technical details about temporal-energy balances and entropic shock waves. Just take it on faith that your concept of parallel universes is a gross oversimplification of the true situation. Timelines just can't be thought of as parallel!

"Energy considerations are our biggest problem. They keep most of the timelines closed to us. And when a volume of low temporal energy *does* form—what we call a Paratime portal—it is usually limited to an area a few miles square. A portal's life can be measured anywhere from milliseconds to thousands of years. The one between Talador, my home timeline, and the Gestetni Republic, for instance, has been open for over six thousand years. Others come and go intermittently, eventually closing forever as the two timelines drift apart. That's the case with your timeline, Duncan. The portal between our universes opened five years ago. We will remain in intermittent contact for about a thousand years and then go our separate ways."

"So why have you people been skulking around?" I asked.

"Experience. It has taught us caution. Terrible things can happen to a Paratime shuttle once it makes the jump between universes."

"Such as?"

"Oh, a million things. You can spend an hour in a strange universe and return home to find a dozen years have passed . . . or that time has run backward while you were gone . . . or that no time at all has passed. The flow of linear time is highly variable from timeline to timeline. We avoid situations where a large mismatch exists, but every member of the Time Watch can expect to age at a slightly different rate from family and friends.

"Then there are the nasty little surprises that people can pull on you. More than once a shuttle has jumped into an unknown timeline to discover the Earth ruled by powerful barbarians with both the yen and the military might for empire. A thousand years ago a Taladoran shuttle discovered the Dalgiri Empire that way. The discovery cost three cities. including two on my home timeline. Since then all of our efforts have been to contain that pack of wild dogs. They controlled eight timelines when we first met them—twelve now. In the same time we have grown from an alliance of three lines to a confederation of thirty-two. We've almost got them boxed."

"Okay, what about this universe—uh, timeline?" I asked. "What are your plans for us?"

"You mean Europo-American?"

"Europo-American? What's that?"

"That is our name for this timeline. When we first arrived, we surveyed your literature to see what you knew of alternate universes. The name comes, I believe, from a science-fiction classic of the early 1960s. We liked the name so well, we adopted it!"

"And your plans for us?"

"To study you for the moment, perhaps establish diplomatic relations later. I really don't know, Duncan. Such decisions are made on a level much higher than mine."

"And the Dalgiri?"

"Their intentions are obvious. They want to add you to their Empire, probably as slaves. And they'll have that chance in twenty years when a direct portal opens between the Empire and here."

"Leaving us to play Poland to their Hitler and your Churchill!" So far, I didn't like the way this conversation was going.

She nodded. "Considering what happened tonight, the conquest may already be well underway."

"And so you've given up your job as a spy to report what you know."

She smiled. "I guess I deserve that. I'm not really a spy, you know, at least not in the classic sense of the word. I am exactly what I claim to be—a graduate anthropology student working on her thesis. But to answer your question: Yes, this is far more important than my information-gathering function."

I suddenly felt very tired. What had started out as a boring evening with Weasel Martin and the other UFO freaks had turned into something else again. Either I had stumbled into the greatest adventure of all time or else I was in the hands of a certifiable nut. The whole night had been like a dream, and fatigue had worn me down until I could hardly think.

"What's the matter, Duncan?" she asked, her voice a husky whisper. "Don't you believe me?"

"I don't know what to believe. I'm not making any decisions until I get caught up on my sleep."

"A good idea," she said, standing and stretching. Her newly lithe form flickered in the firelight.

"You take the bedroom and I'll take the couch," I said.

She smiled broadly and grasped her sweater at the hem, pulling it quickly over her head. My mouth dropped open at the sight of her. *Where had I ever gotten the notion that Jane Dugway was flat-chested?*

"No need for false chivalry, Duncan. My culture is not your culture and I have been celibate much too long in this charade I have been playing."

She turned and walked into the bedroom, her naked back beckoning me. After a moment's tussle with my conscience, I gave in and followed. Suddenly the thought of not getting to sleep for another couple of hours didn't bother me at all.

I woke to the sensations of a winter morning; the drip of melting snow running from the roof, the smell of breakfast on the stove, the heat of pine-speckled sunshine across my upper body. I smiled and stretched and opened my eyes. I was alone. I could hear Jane in the other room. By the elevation of the sun shining through the bedroom window, I judged the time to be around ten o'clock in the morning.

I raised myself up on one elbow and yelled, "Where are you, woman?"

She came to the door wearing oversized Levi's and a flannel shirt. "Morning, sleepyhead. I borrowed some of your uncle's clothes. I hope he won't mind."

"Uncle's a pussycat, at least where beautiful women are concerned." She blushed. I was surprised to realize that I really meant the compliment.

"I suppose I should let you in on one more little secret," she said.

"You're married?"

"No, agents of the Time Watch seldom marry, not even each other. Our lives are too fluid to make such a lasting commitment to another. I'm afraid we are married to our jobs."

"You're a boy!" I said, mock horror on my face.

She laughed. "You have ample proof that I am not, Sir Gallant!"

"I give up."

"My name is not Jane Dugway."

Now it was my turn to smile. "I thought that was a bit too convenient. Okay, I'm braced for it. Let me have it with both barrels!"

"The closest an English-speaking tongue can come to wrapping itself around my true moniker is Jana Dougwaix."

I said it twice, savoring the way the syllables bounced around inside my mouth. "I like it. When do we eat?"

"Breakfast is almost ready. Why don't you get dressed? Lots to do today. We have to be up on the Rim by full dark. The shuttle could make the jump anytime after dusk."

She went back into the kitchen while I dressed. I put on the same clothes I had worn the day before, feeling slightly itchy at the prospect. I wished the water had been turned on. I could have used a bath. Running a hand across my chin, I scraped over the day's growth of beard. My tongue caressed slimy teeth. In spite of my general slovenliness, I felt pretty good. Some of the mental haze that had plagued me since things had started was gone.

Jane/Jana ladled pancakes onto a plate as I came out of the bedroom. I crossed over to where she stood and nibbled on her ear. She giggled just like any red-blooded American girl. You'd never know to look at her that she was a creature from another universe. I let my hands roam lovingly.

There was a sharp rap on the door.

Jana stiffened in my arms. "Who's that?"

I tried to keep my voice light. "Probably just the neighbors from across the meadow. They've seen the smoke and come over to get the latest gossip. It gets damned lonely up here in the winter."

She looked around frantically. "The beamers?"

Now it was my turn to be startled. *The beamers!* What had I done with them? Then I remembered. They'd chafed me when tucked into my belt. So when we got back to the rooming house I transferred them to the pockets of my leather jacket—the jacket that I'd taken off in the generator shack and which still hung on a nail out there.

"Out back," I said, hooking a thumb in that direction. "Don't worry, I'll get rid of our visitors."

"Duncan Allen MacElroy?" the man standing on the porch asked.

I didn't bother to answer. There didn't seem a need.

The stranger was short and squat, with overhanging eyebrows. His wide smile showed a row of jagged teeth. Those weren't his most noticeable features, however. The beamer he held in my face guaranteed that I barely noticed his physical peculiarities.

CHAPTER 3

I stood paralyzed for a moment that seemed as if it would never end. From somewhere behind me came the tinkle of broken glass, followed an instant later by Jana's scream. I whirled around as a second Dalgir leveled his beamer at her through the broken window.

After that, things seemed like a dream again.

In a matter of minutes three Dalgiri—one had been hiding out back in case we'd made a run for it—had searched us with a brusque, impersonal efficiency and frog-marched us into the bedroom. I was ordered to turn and face the wall, then heard a scuffle behind me. When I was allowed to turn back. Jana lay face up on the rumpled bed. Her body was limp, her violet eyes gazed at the ceiling.

Then two of them grabbed my arms and the third applied a shiny steel box to my neck. A sharp prick, and I too was limp all over. It was as if my body had gone to sleep from the neck down. The two Dalgiri brusquely tossed me on the bed beside Jana then left the room.

From then on I saw nothing but the flyspecks on the ceiling, although I had no trouble hearing our guests in the next room. They'd left the door open to keep an eye on us.

"Jana?" I asked softly. My mouth and eyelids were about the only things that still worked.

"Yes, Duncan."

"What happens now?"

Just then the Dalgiri started speaking to each other in rapid-fire gibberish that reminded me of an orchestra tuning up. I heard a brief *"Shush!"* from Jana. She listened intently.

After five minutes the conversation quieted down and one of them glanced in at us. I waited for him to disappear then whispered to Jana, "What was that all about?"

"It's bad, Duncan. Very bad. They've got a Paratime communicator and are using it to call in one of their . . . call it a cruiser. It's an armed shuttle with a crew of two hundred. It's second in firepower only to our biggest warships."

"What for?"

"To ambush our transport when it arrives. This mission is very important to them for some reason. I was right last night. They crossed over to this timeline through the Confederation—my home timeline of Talador, in fact. The cruiser must come the same way. Their transport must have been small enough to slip through our defenses without being observed. The cruiser has no chance of escaping detection. A lot of people at home will die tonight."

"What are we going to do about it?"

A short sob escaped from her throat. "What can we do?"

If my shoulder muscles had been free to move, I'd have shrugged. It didn't look as if there was much we *could* do.

"If only we had the beamers, Duncan."

I felt a brief flash of anger at being so stupid. Then I savagely put the thought from my mind. There had been no reason to think they'd trail us here.

"Look, Jana—if we'd been armed, we would now be dead. You saw the way they were deployed when they jumped us!"

"Maybe we could have won a firefight. Now we'll never know because the beamers are out with the generator."

My mind began to race. I recalled several previous visits to my uncle's cabin. It was then that I smiled. Not being hooked into the power grid was a real pain in the ass. You were forever having to go out and pump some more gas into the generator's fuel tank. For years, Uncle had planned to build a reserve tank out of an old fifty-five-gallon drum. But he'd never gotten around to it.

That meant the generator had fuel for only eight hours

or so, even at the idle setting it used when there was no electrical load on the line. "What time is it?"

"About eleven. Why?"

I listened to the far-off *put-put-put* of the generator. It was a sound that I'd not consciously heard since last night, even though it had been there all the time. Now it seemed louder. I licked my lips and waited, listening for the noise to stop.

I waited for an eternity that probably lasted only fifteen minutes. Finally, it came. The soft chugging of the generator ceased, bringing with it a silence louder than the noise it made when running.

A Dalgir was in the bedroom in seconds.

"What has happened?" he asked.

"Generator's out of fuel. Looks like you boys are going to get cold," I said.

"Never mind that. We need power for our communications beacon. How do we get it back?"

"Know anything about cantankerous internal-combustion engines?"

"I'm no barbarian," he growled.

"Then you'd better let me up so I can go get it started again."

He turned and yelled: "Rimbrick!" A second Dalgir, the leader by his demeanor, came into the bedroom and leveled a beamer at me. There was a sharp prick on my neck, then fire coursed downward through my body. My arms and legs began to twitch uncontrollably.

When the spasm had passed they helped me to stand. I walked around the kitchen to loosen up a bit. Finally the leader turned to the other Dalgir and said something I didn't understand, but which sounded like a command, before ushering me out the back door. We crunched our way to the generator shack.

Once inside, I set to work refilling the tank with gasoline, using an empty mayonnaise jar to transfer it from the storage barrel to the fuel tank. When the generator was topped off I filled the jar once more for good measure. Rimbrick stood warily two arm lengths out of reach in the doorway. I set the gasoline down next to the generator and began to putter around the mechanism. Then I picked up the jar in my left hand and leaned over to the big knife switch on the wall.

"Got to disconnect the load before I start it," I said, throwing the switch. My body shielded my right hand from view as I straightened up, brushing against the coat on the wall. I waited breathlessly for the bolt of lightning to strike my back. Nothing happened. I reached into the jacket pocket and felt the cold handle of a beamer. Praying the safety was off, I mentally judged my distance from the doorway and whirled, throwing the gasoline in one quick motion.

It caught him full in the face. He screamed, instinctively reaching upward to cover his eyes. Then he realized his mistake and brought the beamer down to bear on my chest.

The hesitation was enough. I pointed my weapon at him and pulled the firing stud. There was a crash of light and the overwhelming stink of ozone. When I could open my eyes again, Rimbrick was down in the snow with the familiar hole burned through him. The gasoline had caught fire. Flames and a thin stream of black smoke flickered upward from his jacket.

I quickly grabbed the second beamer and headed for the cabin. I pushed the back door open and padded across the linoleum to the door opening on the living room. I hesitated. It had suddenly occurred to me that I couldn't answer a very basic question. Exactly whose side was I on? True, circumstances seemed to have thrown me in league with Jane Dugway (*a.k.a.* Jana Dougwaix), but was that what *I* wanted? She had killed the Dalgir without warning last night. What if she was with the bad guys and these Dalgiri represented the forces of law and order? Did the concept of good guys and bad guys even apply to a war that had been going on for a thousand years? What was an innocent bystander such as myself doing mixed up in this mess, anyway?

I pushed open the door to the living room, indecision laying on my shoulders like a sack of wet concrete. I'm not sure exactly what it was that I planned. Perhaps they would surrender if I got the drop on them. With the Dalgiri my prisoners and Jana still drugged from the neck down, maybe I could sort things out.

The door squeaked slightly as it opened. Suddenly the whole question of right and wrong became academic. The first Dalgir, the one who had come to see what was wrong when the generator quit, faced me from across the room. Surprise flashed across his features as he lunged for his beamer.

I shot him—and the other one when he tried to quick-draw against me as well.

Then I sat down and was quietly sick for a few minutes. Later I released Jana, following her instructions on how to administer the antidote to the drug they'd given us.

She wasted no time heading for the communicator. She did something incomprehensible to the controls and then cursed softly under her breath. Turning to look at me, she smiled sheepishly.

"Darling, would you mind turning the electricity back on? They've drained their power cells."

I grinned. "Sure thing, boss."

I trudged back to the generator and quickly had it going again. When I returned to the cabin, Jana had just finished talking into the thing that looked like a portable radio. She turned to look gravely at me.

"Well?"

"Made it. I can't use this thing to talk across timelines without the Dalgiri hearing, but I did get our office in New York. They'll relay the message and that cruiser will have a big surprise waiting when it tries to cross over tonight. Funny, though."

"What?"

"This communicator. It wasn't tuned to the crosstime settings at all. I found it on the local . . . uh, channels."

"That important?"

She sighed. "Probably not."

"What do we do now?"

"We wait here. The shuttle will come through right after dark to pick us up."

"Us?"

A strange look came over her face, as if she were seeing me for the first time. Then she was in my arms.

"They could have killed us while we lay helpless in there," she said between sobs.

I held her, softly caressing the back of her neck. "Why didn't they?" I asked.

She lifted her head from my shoulder and dried her tears. "Because of you."

"Me?"

"Never mind just now," she said, sniffing. "There is something we must talk about."

We sat on the couch. I reached over to take her in my arms, but she pushed me away.

"Don't. You can't afford to have your mind clouded with emotion just now. You've a decision to make, the most important of your life."

"What decision?"

She gulped and regarded me with red eyes. "Whether you will submit voluntarily to having your memories of the last day erased, or will exile yourself from this timeline forever."

"I don't understand."

"Don't you see? You know about Paratime! It's standard procedure in cases like this to memory-wipe any local who learns of our existence."

"That's gratitude for you." I could feel the flush rising in my cheeks. Maybe I *had* picked the wrong side in this war.

"I know, Duncan. It's wrong! But civilizations sometimes can't afford the luxury of gratitude. It's a cruel universe out there. In fact, there are thousands of cruel universes out there. Sometimes we don't have any choice."

"I don't suppose it would do any good to conk you on the head and make a run for it," I said.

She shook her head. "I reported your being with me when I called from the rooming house. Within a few weeks they would hunt you down and you'd lose an even bigger chunk of memory."

"And exile?"

"You could join us, Duncan. The Time Watch always needs good people. We patrol a hundred different universes and there are never enough Watchmen to go around."

"I don't care much for being drafted, Jana."

"Nobody does."

"For one thing, I'm not sure you people are right in all of this."

"All of what?"

"Your war with the Dalgiri. You *did* fire the first shot—and without warning—you know."

Jana's face darkened. It was as if a volcano was getting ready to erupt. She sat, considering her reply, for a dozen seconds. Then she exploded.

"You're damned lucky that I did, Duncan MacElroy!"

"Huh?"

"Don't you see? How did that Dalgir track me down at your rooming house? And the three others found us here at your uncle's cabin. How? How could they possibly have known where we were?"

I shrugged. *"Damfino*. Haven't had much time to think about it."

"They found us because they were *looking for you*, Duncan, not me!"

"I don't understand. Why would they be looking for me?"

"Because they were from our future, stupid! Sometime in the next fifty years you are going to become a major stumbling block in the path of the Dalgiri Empire. So much so that they will mount an expedition across time-lines—one aimed at you *personally*. They found us so easily because they have studied your life since early childhood. The only thing that saved you was my chancing to spot that aversion field. Otherwise you'd be dead."

"From the future?" I mumbled stupidly about ten times.

"Yes, from the future," she said, finally. "The five-dimensional surface that describes Paratime is convoluted beyond belief. Travel into the past is completely feasible —if you're willing to spend a few years waiting on a skewed timeline for the right portal to open up. There are timelines without number where time flows in reverse."

"Then it must have taken them years," I said.

"Probably—decades if they were willing to spend them in cold sleep. But you are important to them. Important enough to expend four field agents and a cruiser in the attempt. That makes you important to us."

I couldn't think of anything to say.

"Well?" she asked.

"Well, I'll be damned!"

"You certainly will."

The transport shuttle came through at full dark, guided to the cabin by the Dalgiri homer. It was an ebon egg some ten yards long that hovered a foot off the snowpack. The three-man crew was briskly efficient. Within minutes they had loaded the dead into a cargo hold and begun to clean up all evidence of the fight in and around the cabin. I wrote a note to Tony Minetti, explaining that the stranger returning his jeep was my cousin and asking him to hand over my Jag. I wrote another to Hal Benson, telling him to forward my clothes and stereo to an address in New York City. I wondered briefly what he would think of the three crisp hundred-dollar bills I enclosed in the envelope. Then it was out to the generator shack to kill the power for the last time.

Finally, it was time to go. The field agent pulled away from the cabin in the jeep. Jana and I watched the red taillights out of sight before we turned and walked arm in arm toward the rectangle of blue light spilling from the shuttle's open hatch.

Suddenly the confusion, fear, and fatigue that had plagued me for the last twenty-four hours were gone. A feeling of exhilaration washed over me. It was the exhilaration of being alive and on the threshold of a great adventure. Of being nine feet tall and covered with hair, and ready to buckle my swash from one end of Paratime to the other. Of having seen the future and discovered greatness there.

"I'm sorry I called you stupid," Jana said, snuggling close as we walked.

"You're not the first." Suddenly I stopped in my tracks. A funny thought had just hit me.

"What's the matter?"

"Your shuttle," I said with a chuckle.

"What about it?"

"I just realized. Joel Peterson was right! UFOs *are* ships from another universe." Then I laughed. What started as a chuckle built quickly into a belly-jiggling guffaw. I laughed so hard tears began to run down my cheek.

Suddenly Jana was laughing, too.

When she'd finally managed to get control of herself, she wiped the tears from her eyes. "I don't know how to tell you this, Duncan. UFOs *really are* swamp gas! Or weather balloons, or airplane lights, or St. Elmo's fire. We shield our shuttles with aversion fields. They are practically invisible at night. There hasn't been a sighting of one of our ships in the whole five years we have been operating on this timeline."

I turned to stare at her. "Really?"

She nodded.

"Well, I *will* be damned!"

Then we started to laugh again. This time the joke was even funnier.

CHAPTER 4

My first glimpse of Talador was via the forward viewscreen as the transport shuttle touched down at Jafta Port, the main terminus for traffic to and from the capital city of the Taladoran Confederation. Talador is the focal point for the trade of a hundred alternate Earths, giving Jafta Port an ambience instantly recognizable to anyone who had ever sailed into a major deep-water harbor or changed planes at a large international airport. It reminded me of what JFK in New York will probably look like in a thousand years—only bigger.

Jana didn't give me time to sightsee on the ramp. She ushered me into a two-person car instead, a robot conveyance that whisked us through a dizzying series of tunnels, past rushing throngs of humanity, up a series of ramps, and finally braked to a stop in bright sunlight on a rooftop. I followed her out of the car, feeling more than a little wobbly in the knees. In less than a minute we had traveled nearly two miles and my senses had been assaulted by sights, sounds, and smells unlike any I had ever experienced. I suppose I should have been alive with the excitement of it all. I wasn't.

I was scared.

It was beginning to sink in that there would be no return from this voyage of discovery. I had plunged off the high board and was only now checking to see if the pool held any water.

Jana must have seen the blood drain from my face and my knees begin to shake, because she slipped her arm through mine and snuggled up close.

"Do you want to go back inside, Duncan?"

"Don't mind me," I said, shivering. "I'll get over it in time—say a year or two."

We walked arm in arm to a waist-high railing that ran along the edge of the rooftop. I gasped. Below me was a cubic mile of air and little else. Yet even from just shy of the clouds, Jafta Port stretched nearly to the horizon in every direction. And everywhere I looked, my gaze fell upon the myriad ships of Paratime.

There were huge globes, medium-size saucers, small and not so small cones, arrows, cubes, black eggs like the one I had arrived in, and other shapes not so easily categorized. Gnat-size aircars glided silently into and out of sight while at the extreme range of vision were two immense shapes that Jana said were dreadnoughts of the Taladoran Navy.

"Wow!" I whispered reverently, trying to take in everything at once, my fear nearly forgotten. Suddenly I was just a rubbernecker, eyes about to burst and mouth agape with the wonder of it all.

Jana smiled, luxuriating in my reaction to my first sight of her hometown. "Impressive, isn't it?"

"How do you do it?"

"Do what?"

"How can you possibly maintain such a civilization after having been at war with Dalgir for a thousand years? Your economy should have collapsed ages ago!"

She laughed. "Our 'economy' is a complex machine, not easily damaged. As for our war with the Empire, we have been at it so long that it is part of our lives. We have figured it into the 'equations.'" She went on with what I'm sure she thought was a simple explanation of the whole process. I listened carefully, nodded politely, and didn't understand a single word.

"Sounds a bit like the village idiot and his cannon," I said finally when she was through.

"I don't understand, Duncan."

So I told her the joke about the town council that wanted to give the village idiot something to do for his welfare check. After thinking on the problem awhile, they decide to hire him to polish the cannon on the courthouse lawn every Saturday. Years pass and one day the idiot gives notice that he is quitting. "Why?" the councilmen

ask. "Because I've saved my money all these years, and
have finally gotten enough to go into business for myself.
I just bought my own cannon!"

Jana's laugh *sounded* genuine, but I still found it hard to
believe that the joke was new to a civilization encom-
passing thirty-two alternate Earths.

Eventually, I tired of craning my neck this way and
that, and Jana took me down into the building below us.
We ended up inside a concourse big enough to have
weather. There she guided me into one of the "gnat-size"
aircars—that turned out to be slightly bigger than a 1958
Cadillac—and programmed it for Time Watch Headquarters.

I spent the next two months being poked, prodded,
questioned, inoculated, indoctrinated, pinched, studied,
and having things done to me that were just plain incomprehensible. Most of my time was spent hooked up to education machines of one kind or another. Most pumped
knowledge into me by a process that looked like hypnosis,
but wasn't. And just because I was in a state of trancelike
concentration during the lessons didn't mean that the
learning came easy.

First was Temporal Basic—the *lingua franca* of the
Time Watch. When I had the basics of that liquidly musi-
cal language mastered, they started me on the hard stuff.

One of my first lessons after Temporal Basic was in the
organization, purposes, and traditions of the Taladoran
Time Watch. In many ways, it was similar to the quick
"economics lesson" Jana had tried to give me. The words
were all there, but the basic structure needed for understanding the concepts had yet to be erected. It was as if
each fact had to be filed in a pigeonhole in my gray matter, but I had yet to drill the pigeonholes to file them in.

So I fell back on analogy. The Watch is a military organization of sorts, but then again, it isn't. Talador has
both an army and a navy, with the prime responsibility
for providing the military might that keeps the Dalgiri at
bay. But then, the Time Watch has some kind of fuzzy
responsibility over the army and navy, acting as an elite
corps of specialists who direct operations.

Each timeline in the Confederation has its own laws

and police powers, a practice Talador learned over the ages that other Paratime Civilizations frequently had not. Each timeline of the Confederation was an entire planet —each with its own history, customs, mores, and traditions. Such a situation requires a good deal of flexibility and home rule. But the Watch had police powers, too. It was responsible for policing all crosstime traffic to make sure that unscrupulous citizens of one timeline didn't take advantage of the inhabitants of another.

And, of course, the Time Watch ran the Taladoran espionage and diplomatic services. A Watchman could find himself anywhere in the known universes, doing almost anything. It was an elite service, and one few could qualify for. I was beginning to wonder if I had what it takes.

Not all of my teachers were machines, of course. I found myself meeting at all hours of the day and night with a bewildering variety of people. After a while I began to suspect that some of them were Very Important People indeed!

Mostly such sessions ran together in my mind. All except the last one . . .

It had been nearly six weeks since I had been separated from Jana and turned over to my teachers—keepers?— and their machines. By that time my head felt as if it would split if forced to memorize even a single additional fact. I was notified that I was to report to Capitol Complex right after breakfast.

Capitol Complex turned out to be a city within a city, a single edifice so huge that it dwarfed even Jafta Port. I was met by a Taladoran naval officer—at least an admiral to judge by his uniform—who guided me through a maze that would have made the mad geniuses who built the Pentagon envious. He handed me off to someone of even higher rank, who guided me to what had to be the Chairman of the Joint Chiefs, who guided me to someone more exalted still!

By the time I was ushered into an anteroom the size of a football field, I was deeply engrossed in guessing how long the escalation could go on. I was ushered immediately into the *sanctum sanctorum*.

I found Jana inside, seated before the desk of a silver-haired man with a harried look about him. Something about her expression restrained me from yelling for joy and hugging her until she turned blue. Instead I moved hesitantly to stand before the dignitary's desk.

Jana did the honors: "Duncan, I would like to introduce Tasloss Vios of the Oulra Timeline, the Speaker of the Ruling Council."

"Honored, sir," I said, bowing in what I hoped was the proper form. I may have been a hayseed from the boondocks, but I wasn't so ignorant that I hadn't heard of the Ruling Council.

"It is I who am honored, Mr. MacElroy. Please be seated." Tasloss spoke English with a curious accent. That he had learned it quite recently—say, that morning—was obvious. That he had bothered to learn it at all was amazing.

"Thank you, sir."

"Watchman Dougwaix reported the circumstances of your case upon her return from Europo-American. Since that time I have found an inordinate amount of the Confederation's all-too-valuable manpower and computer time taken up with the matter. To put it bluntly, we wondered if you are truly what you appear to be."

"I beg your pardon, sir?"

"Consider the problem from our side, Mr. MacElroy. You are an outtime aborigine, born and raised on a timeline that lacks any crosstime capability whatsoever. Prior to two months ago, you knew nothing of either Talador or Dalgir. Yet on the night that you just happened to be in the company of one of the handful of Taladoran agents on your timeline, you were attacked by a Dalgiri assassination team from the future. What is the probability of such a thing happening?"

My voice was a hoarse whisper as I answered, "Not very high, sir."

Tasloss regarded me with what I took to be suspicious eyes. "Not very high, indeed! The whole idea is preposterous! It is a practical impossibility! To believe your story is to believe that someone has drawn consecutive royal flushes with an honest deck. A much more likely explanation of the episode is that it is merely a Dalgiri plot arranged for our benefit. Perhaps the purpose was to place a spy in our midst."

My heart lurched. "A spy? Me?"

"Who else? Yet, we have discovered a great deal about you in the last several months. We know that your parents brought you home from the hospital a week late—a serious case of postpartum jaundice, I believe. Then there was that embarrassing day when you wet your pants in the third grade. Or I could give you the name of the young lady who taught you the facts of life when you were fourteen."

I gulped again.

"However, though it offends my sense of order and logic, I am forced to conclude that you are exactly what you appear to be."

"Which is?" I asked.

"Why, a gift from the gods, of course! A solid-gold, brass-bound, genuine article; an opportunity to gain the upper hand over Dalgir once and for all. You are absolute proof that we shall someday triumph over those devils. Why else would they go to so much trouble to kill you?"

I shrugged. Personally, I had my doubts about being anything special, but I was in no position to argue just yet.

Tasloss turned to Jana and winked. I had learned enough to know that it was a completely artificial gesture for a Taladoran, one obviously adopted for my benefit. "You tell him, Watchman."

Jana, who had refused to meet my gaze almost since the meeting began, suddenly smiled. "You have been ordered to the Time Watch Academy on Salfa Prime."

"Right now?" I asked.

Tasloss guffawed. "Would ten days R & R help?—that was the correct expression, was it not?"

"Yes, sir, on both counts," I said.

"Would you like to share it with him, Jana?"

"Very much, Tasloss." She grinned.

"Then get out of my office. I've work to do."

We got!

Jana and I spent ten glorious days exploring Jafta and its analogs on neighboring timelines. We never traveled very far in miles—usually just to the shuttle port and back

—but what we lacked in distance, we more than made up in variety. At the end of our leave, we spent a tender night and a morning of tearful good-byes.

"Will you write to me?" I asked as we embraced for one last time at the shuttle port.

"Of course," she said, tears streaming down her cheeks.

I reached out to touch her cheek. "Come on now. What are those for?"

She sniffed. "I'm always like this. What do you say to a good friend you may never see again?"

"We'll get together sometime."

She shook her head. "You don't have any idea how many people there are in the Confederation, or how thinly the Watch is stretched, Duncan."

"I'll make an effort to find you," I said.

"No! Let's cherish what we have had together, but don't make any promises we can't keep. Remember what I told you that morning in your uncle's cabin. A Watchman can't afford permanent attachments."

"Meaning?"

"Meaning that I have no permanent hold on you, nor you on me. We are comrades-in-arms, nothing more."

I thought about it for a while, then probed my psyche for the wounds of rejection. Surprisingly, there weren't any. I grinned and shrugged. "But you *will* write, won't you?"

"Of course, I will!"

"Then how about one more kiss for an old comrade— oof! Why did you hit me?"

"For making jokes and spoiling our good-bye!"

Imagine a school that combines all the military tradition of West Point, St. Cyr, and Sandhurst with the scholarship of Harvard, Oxford, and Cal Tech, and you will have some idea of what the Time Watch Academy is like.

In one respect I was lucky. I had expected to suffer a serious bout of melancholia following my arrival on Salfa Prime. After all, I was now cut off from everything that I had ever known. Even Jana was gone. Shortly after my arrival she wrote to tell me she had been reassigned to Europo-American to continue her interrupted studies. I was all alone, as alone as any exile in the history of my world.

Funny, I didn't notice. I didn't notice because my instructors never gave me a chance to. I don't think I had more than ten minutes' spare time in my first six months at the Academy. Partly, of course, that was the idea. All of the neophyte Watchmen-in-Training had been isolated from their native cultures and would have had a tendency to brood, given the opportunity.

And, besides, my case was special because the amount of knowledge I needed to soak up was staggering. Not just the esoteric subjects necessary to operate successfully across the hundreds of timelines then open to the Confederation, but also the kindergarten things every Taladoran learned before he could walk. I was the South Sea Island savage who suddenly found himself in the great courts of Europe, not exactly sure how he got there or how he was going to get home again. Except I wasn't going home . . . ever!

Mornings at the Academy were devoted to working up a sweat. Up at Twenty—the Taladorans break the day into one hundred bora—we were out on the exercise fields before sunrise. Next came combat training. Come Fifty and we broke for a quick meal, followed by an afternoon of skull sweat. Evenings were usually spent in the central library or in a laboratory.

Usually that meant boning up on the day's lecture in temporal physics: "It all started with the Big Bang, the cosmic explosion that shattered all of space, rending the great primal egg into a near infinity of stars and galaxies. Matter and energy were violently ejected across billions of light-years, and even time itself was wrenched asunder.

"In that steaming cauldron of chemical, nuclear, and temporal reactions, Paratime was born.

"An observer standing outside, equipped to see the Universe's five-dimensional shape, would probably look down on a glowing starburst, each timeline radiating outward from the single brilliant center. But as the shape of a spiral galaxy is much simpler to comprehend when viewed from outside, so too the shape of Paratime. To the uncounted trillions of intelligent beings trapped inside, the symmetry of the lines is far from apparent. From within, the structure of the separate universes is chaotic, random, unformed.

"Most civilizations develop the concept of 'parallel universes' shortly after inventing the scientific method. They usually visualize the timelines as a series of recordstrips laid side by side, each stretching neatly from the very beginnings of time into the infinite future. Each universe is a near-identical reproduction of the universes to either side. Travel from one timeline to another—if thought possible at all—is a journey through a series of increasingly remote probabilities, with the degree of difference between where you are and where you came from a measure of the number of universes that lie between. As a philosophical model this concept is elegant in the extreme. Elegant, but wrong.

"A culture has taken the first steps down the path to crosstime travel when its philosophers realize that rather than being parallel, the alternate universes tend to touch, and interpenetrate, and separate again with maddening irregularity. And, effectively infinite in number—if not also in actuality—it is inevitable that there exists in every universe a point that is congruent to a corresponding point in one of the other universes. And wherever this congruence exists, for however long a span of linear time, a 'gate' exists between worlds, a portal for those with the knowledge to use it."

The teaching machine's dry whisper inside my skull lulled me to sleep more nights than not. For if I thought quantum mechanics had been difficult, it was a mere kindergarten exercise compared to the science of Paratime.

Eventually the killing load of the academic and physical training slacked off a bit. Whether this was by design of the powers-that-be, or merely a sign that I was beginning to learn, I was never truly sure. Not that I ever found myself at loose ends for hours at a time. But occasionally, every other Tenday or so, I managed to catch up enough to take a few hours off.

CHAPTER 5

"COME on in, the water's fine."

The sun was warm on my body as I lay on the granite outcrop that overlooked the forest pool. Haret was a flesh-colored streak in a pool of amber green, keeping herself afloat by treading water as she taunted me to return to the icy stream.

I raised my head from my arms, admiring the way her figure shimmered beneath the surface of the pond. "No way," I said. "Too cold. You come out."

"Coward!"

I grinned. "Sticks and stones will break my bones—" My taunt was interrupted by a cloud of icy spray propelled with unerring accuracy by Haret's strong right arm. The freezing droplets splashed across my toasty-warm back, sending chills clear to my toes. I launched myself in a flat racing dive. Within seconds I had grappled her flailing arms, pinned them to her body, and pulled her head beneath the wavelets of the pond.

We surfaced sputtering and swam leisurely for the shore. I helped her climb the slippery mud bank and we stretched out side by side on the spot I had so recently vacated.

Haret Ryland was a native of the Gestetni Republic, one of the Confederation's three oldest timelines. She was on the Academy staff, and, like Jana, an expert in Para-time anthropology. She had asked to interview me about Europo-American my second day on Salfa Prime. That had been the first of many such sessions. We became close friends over the next eighteen months. Recently, our friendship drifted into intimacy.

I reached out and idly traced the curve of Haret's naked spine with a finger, caressing each vertebra in turn until I had worked my way down to the swell of her hips.

"Stop that." She giggled as she turned over to allow the sun a chance to dry her front. "It tickles."

"I thought you liked being tickled." I reached out once more.

She intercepted my questing hand with a playful slap. "Don't you primitive types ever get enough?"

I put on my most theatrical leer. "Never!"

She hoisted herself to one elbow, her violet-tinged eyes staring into mine.

"What's the matter?" I asked. "Is my nose on crooked?"

"Isn't everyone's?"

She fell silent, letting her eyes roam. Her full mouth was pursed in concentration, and her normally wild mane of silky blond hair framed her face in a wet tangle.

"Why the sudden quiet?" I asked, reaching once more to take her in my arms.

"I'm contemplating an enigma."

"Huh? What enigma?"

"You. What brings you to the Time Watch, Duncan MacElroy?"

"You know damned well what brings me to the Watch. I was drafted!"

She grinned. "That isn't what I meant. Don't you ever miss your former life?"

"Sometimes. But if I'd stayed on Europo-American, I would never have met you." I leaned toward her as I spoke and brushed her lips with mine.

Haret took my cue. She closed her eyes with a sigh and stretched out on the flat rock as I pressed close, intent on pursuing the emotion of the moment.

The sky above us lit up with a light brighter than a thousand suns.

Haret's eyes snapped open in fright and I began counting softly to myself. I had reached fifty when the rumble of deep-throated thunder rolled over us.

"Dalgiri!" Haret yelled as we scrambled to our feet and ran for our aircar.

I didn't have to ask what she meant. Anyone who can remember the Cold War of the late fifties and early sixties knows instinctively what that flash in the sky means. We had seen a nuclear weapon burst somewhere to the south.

"They must be after the portal," I said, panting as we reached the aircar and began throwing on our uniforms.

"Impossible," Haret said. "The Academy can't be reached from any Dalgiri timeline."

I realized that she was right. Salfa Prime was a cul-de-sac in the structure of Paratime. There was but a single portal, and that led back through a companion universe—Salfa Null—to one of the Confederation's outlying time-lines. The only way in or out was through the closely knit universes of the Confederation.

I glanced away from the south as another brilliant flash lit the sky. This time the thunder rolled over us just thirty seconds later. I looked northward, toward the Academy, and wondered why no mushroom clouds had sprouted in that direction. The Academy had to be the raiders' target.

We wasted not an instant longer as we leaped into the aircar and Haret lifted it from the forest glen.

"Where to?" she asked.

I glanced over the green hills and valleys of what should have been Central Africa, but wasn't. Wilderness stretched for as far as the eye could see—and considerably farther. The only human beings on this timeline were at the Academy.

"Home to the Academy," I said. "Let's just hope it survives long enough for us to get there."

"Let's hope it survives a lot longer than that, Duncan." She sent the aircar screaming north at full power.

We bucked our way through wicked thermals as we raced for home, the twin pillars of destruction clearly visible in the rear viewscreen. The Dalgiri shuttle was a tiny black speck moving away from us toward the invisible volume of space that was the temporal portal between this timeline and the next. Whether it did so in retreat or attack was impossible to say.

I stepped up the magnification until the shuttle was a black circle against the brilliant blue of the sky. Suddenly a dozen specks materialized in the open sky around it. My heart sank to my socks as I realized we were as good as dead. Thirteen Dalgiri shuttles could carry enough firepower to make Salfa Prime uninhabitable for the rest of eternity.

I had time to gulp once before something flashed behind us, more brilliant than the others by an order of magnitude, and the viewscreen burned out. My head and shoulders were suddenly aflame where they projected above the curve of the aircar body. Haret screamed as the lift-and-drive generators ceased their quiet hum and the car fell free toward the clear blue of a mountain lake.

I opened my mouth to yell as the aircar's nose burrowed into the blue wet and icy cold engulfed me once more.

The car bobbed to the surface almost as quickly as it had taken the plunge, its interior awash in molten ice courtesy of the open window on Haret's side. I moved quickly to unsnap my safety harness. Haret did likewise. Then, as the engine compartment and storage spaces began to fill with water, I grabbed the emergency kit from under the seat while Haret forced the door open.

We kicked our way out into the bitter cold of the lake just as the car turned nose down and headed for the bottom.

We were chilled to the bone by the time we finished the hundred-yard swim to shore. The water seemed colder than at our swimming pond, even though the streams that fed both originated in the snows of the same mountain range to the east.

Once ashore, we took turns bandaging each other's injuries and smearing evil-smelling yellow salve on our burns. Luckily, our injuries were minor. I had a sprained shoulder and a couple of tender ribs where the harness cut into me. Haret's forehead was gashed where she had struck the aircar's instrument panel. We had been lucky in the burn department too, just a little singed around the edges. My singes were worse than Haret's because of my darker hair. By the time we had stripped off our wet uniforms, started a fire, treated our injuries, dried our uniforms and put them back on, the anesthetic in the salve was at work and I had begun to feel almost human.

"What happened?" I asked as Haret sorted through the

emergency kit. It was strictly a first-aid kit, without a communicator.

"Disrupter beam burned out the lift-and-drive. Luckily for us, the fail-safe worked long enough to cushion the blow."

"What now?"

She tilted her head to one side in the gesture that replaces the shrug among Taladorans. "Either we stay here and wait for rescue or we walk."

"Rescue while the Dalgiri are establishing their beachhead?"

"Right. I guess we walk."

It took two days to hike to the Academy. All that first day, we hid whenever air traffic went over, fearful of being spotted on the ground by the Dalgiri. One of the required courses at the Academy was intended to convince us that the Dalgiri were not nice people. The instructors had succeeded all too well as far as I was concerned. Students had been known to faint during lectures on Dalgiri customs as they applied to captive timelines.

The next morning we gave up trying to hide from the shuttles that flew overhead. For one thing, there were too many of them; lying low was cutting into our travel time. Besides, the shuttles that flitted silently above us all appeared to be Taladoran.

The sun had just disappeared over the western horizon as we limped tiredly out of the hills and down onto the plain where the Academy was built. As soon as we left the tree line for the open grasslands of the savanna an aircar detached itself from the main Academy complex. Haret and I dropped tiredly to our haunches as the car circled overhead and came to a landing a dozen yards in front of us.

The aircar pilot was Ealfor Saouthin, another student and a native of the Praisen timeline. I knew him by sight, but except for polite nods as we passed each other on the way to class, I couldn't remember ever having spoken to him.

"What the hell is going on around here, Ealfor?" I

asked as I got to my feet and brushed the dark loam from my pants. "What were the fireworks about yesterday?"

"A Dalgiri shuttle raided us, of course."

"*A single Dalgir?* What about the other ships we saw?"

"Those were ours. Would I be standing here now if they'd been cragfaces?"

"Then it's all over? We're safe?" Haret asked wearily. The effects of the fifty-mile hike and a fitful night's sleep on the hard ground had taken their toll.

"I would have thought so," Ealfor said, "but apparently not. The order's been given to evacuate Salfa Prime."

"Evacuate? What on Earth for?" I asked.

Ealfor shrugged. "I just follow orders around here. Speaking of which—they've had search parties out looking for you two ever since your aircar was found at the bottom of a lake early this morning. The orders are to find you and get you to Academy H.Q. Let's move!"

With that he loaded us into the aircar and lifted off. I slumped in my seat, resting my head against the car window, my brain in turmoil. Evacuate Salfa Prime? It didn't make sense. A single Dalgiri raider shouldn't have been enough to panic the Taladoran high command into abandoning the Academy.

As we approached the main complex, however, I glanced down into the growing dark and knew that Ealfor had spoken the literal truth.

The Time Watch Academy is more than a place to train new blood for the perennially undermanned Watch. It's also a research center in the field of temporal physics; a place for veteran Watchmen to return and hone their skills; a cultural center where young, able, questing minds can meet, exchange ideas, and develop.

One of the requirements for those who would become Watchmen is full participation in the cultural activities of the Academy's society.

As Ealfor piloted the aircar toward the great inverted pyramid that is Academy H.Q., we passed over a mile-long strip of dark dormitories, cafeterias, laboratories, simulators, and exercise courts. I had spent fully eight nights out of ten over the last year studying at the great central library. Its brilliant façade should have been visible from a hundred miles out. Yet, we passed not fifty feet over the library's roof and the normally scintillating walls were lifeless.

I craned my neck to keep the library in sight as it passed under us. For an instant I stared down into the great plaza fronting it. Normally, the plaza would have been alive with Watchmen-in-Training and strolling couples at ease among the statuary, but the great mall was deserted. No one was visible along its entire length.

Any residual doubt I might have had instantly evaporated. Salfa Prime was definitely being evacuated, and after a raid by only one Dalgiri shuttle. Something was very wrong.

CHAPTER 6

HEADQUARTERS was a tomb compared to the few other times I had been inside. Record boxes were scattered everywhere and the normally immaculate offices showed the effects of a hasty retreat. Everyone we passed seemed to be in a hurry.

Ealfor paid no attention to the pandemonium around him, but led us straight to the grav chute and up to the top floor, where he ushered us into a conference room.

"Wait. I'll tell Watchman Corst that you're here."

I turned to Haret. There was a look of surprise on her face.

"What's the matter?" I asked.

"Dal Corst was an instructor at the Academy when I studied here. If he is involved, it must be important. Last I heard, he was commanding a survey team outtime somewhere."

"Not 'somewhere,' Haret!" a voice boomed from behind us. "I was exploring this young man's home world—and a fascinating place it is."

I turned to see a gray-clad Watchman with a craggy face and a Levantine nose standing with hands on hips behind us. His face wore a broad grin.

"Duncan MacElroy, I presume."

"Yes, sir."

"Don't be so formal. I'm Dal to my friends."

"Thanks, Dal. Were you really on Europo-American?"

"Sure was. Spent the last five years operating out of New York City. Enjoyed the experience immensely. Your people have a lot to be proud of."

"Huh? We're just an average bunch of country bumpkins who haven't tripped over the secret of Paratime travel yet."

"Don't put yourself down. Take your space program and environmentalists, for instance."

"What has one to do with the other?"

"Everything. They are two facets of the same impulse, namely your society's reaction to your lack of crosstime capability. Take your expression: 'There's only one Earth, so we have to take care of it.' Such a thought would never occur to a Taladoran or a Dalgir—especially not to a Dalgir. Why should it? The statement is demonstrably untrue. We have literally thousands of Earths at our disposal. The knowledge that our resources are effectively infinite colors the way we look at things, just as the knowledge of your world's very finite resources colors the way your people view their universe."

I nodded. Jana had shown me some of the Confederation's industrial timelines. The Taladorans considered such alternate Earths expendable resources. Factories dumped their wastes into rivers, metal ore was ripped from the ground in the most efficient and least esthetic manner possible. As for air pollution, the industrial lines had smog problems that just wouldn't quit!

"I don't see what that has to do with space," I said.

"But isn't it obvious? Europo-American is a single timeline on which all the frontiers have been explored. You are a maturing culture with no real horizons. So what do you do? You create your own horizons. Where others turn to Paratime for their frontiers, you have been forced to turn your eyes to the endless vacuum overhead. You've sent men to the Moon. No other timeline we know of has accomplished a similar feat. Why should they? They have an infinity of living, breathing planets to explore. There is no need to send men to that dead pile of rock in the sky. Yet your people did it. That is something to be proud of!"

Looking at it that way, it made sense. The discovery of crosstime travel automatically short-circuited any thought of space exploration. And why not? The alternate Earths had everything mankind could want. There are no other habitable planets in the Solar System, so why invest in the hazardous business of sealing yourself in a vacuum-proof sardine can and spending years getting somewhere that wasn't half as interesting as what you had left?

"If I can find time, I just might write a monograph on the subject," Corst said. "But enough of this theoretical stuff. We've a more practical problem facing us. Please take a seat with a good view of the screen."

Haret and I seated ourselves in two high-back chairs just as the wall screen lit to display a Paratime flow chart, a three-dimensional representation of the relationship between a number of timelines.

Making sense out of a Paratime map is a job for experts —which I was not, not by a long shot. Even so, I recognized the diagram on the screen. It was a representation of the major timelines of the Taladoran Confederation, including the major temporal portals that interconnect them. I recognized it because we had studied that same hologram for fifty bora in Temporal Geopolitics, studied it until I could see it in my sleep.

The Confederation is a classic example of an interdependent timeline cluster, a collection of timelines that move through 5-space more or less in concert—or, as I thought of it, a Paratime galaxy. The mathematics of such clusters are complex beyond belief; and like any student having trouble grasping a difficult concept, I took refuge in analogy.

The way I looked at it, the timelines of the Confederation were akin to the strands of conductor in a telephone cable that has lain too long under the city streets. When the cable was new, each strand formed a distinct and separate circuit. Every circuit was isolated from every other by the surrounding insulation. People whose calls shared the cable were blissfully unaware of the hundreds or thousands of other conversations going on in close proximity to their own.

But as the cable aged, its insulation began to break down in spots. Short circuits appeared and electrical arcs cross-connected the strands of conductor in odd and unpredictable ways. And wherever the electrical arcs had welded the individual strands of cable together, a signal could jump the barrier between circuits. In other words, the places where short circuits formed were the temporal portals of my analogy.

Dal Corst touched a control, and the hologram projected in front of the wall screen changed. It was now a close-up of one section of the original diagram, the section showing the relationship of Salfa Null and Salfa Prime to the home lines of the Confederation.

"The problem is simple," he began without preamble. "The Dalgiri shuttle that raided Salfa Prime yesterday morning did *not* come through this timeline's only portal."

"But that's impossible," Haret said. "It had to."

"Impossible or not, it didn't," Dal replied.

"There must be another portal then. Perhaps one we haven't discovered yet."

"No, we checked. There is only the one."

Haret shut up, a troubled look on her face. I could see what was bothering her. If the Dalgiri shuttle hadn't come through the portal, that meant that the Empire had made a breakthrough. The portals enforced a certain amount of order and predictability on what was otherwise chaos. If the Dalgiri could jump a temporal barrier without a portal, no one throughout Paratime would be safe. Pandora's box was wide open and there was no one to close it again.

"Is that what caused the evacuation order?" I asked.

"Of course. This Academy and the industrial plants next door on Salfa Null represent a major investment in manpower and capital for us. We cannot afford to risk their destruction. Do you know what the loss of twelve thousand Watchmen-in-Training would do to us for the next generation?"

"Then we are defeated," Haret said. "The Dalgiri are free to raid us wherever they wish."

"Maybe," Dal said. "Then again, maybe not. There are some things we do not understand yet about our raider, some points that give us hope."

"Such as?"

"Such as the fact that he quickly destroyed our two fixed batteries guarding the portal, but did not move on the Academy itself until it was too late. It was almost as if he were as surprised to see us as we were to see him."

"So?"

"Why did he appear here if he wasn't expecting a fight?

Maybe he didn't have any choice in the matter because the line he transitioned from is nearby."

"Then he would have had to come from Salfa Null," Haret said. "In terms of overall energy potential, that is the timeline that is closest to this one. But we control Salfa Null, so he couldn't come from there, either."

Dal Corst pressed the screen control once more and a new diagram formed. This one was different from any I had seen before.

"We have been experimenting with computer representations of Paratime recently in the hope of improving our predictions of when and where temporal portals will form. This is such a model of the Salfa Null—Salfa Prime couplet. You will note that these two timelines form an interdependent cluster with a theoretical third line, one to which we do not have access."

I looked at the screen and fixed my gaze on a reddish, twisting worm trail that threaded its way through the green lines of the Confederation and its possessions. Nowhere along the new line's length was the bent trapezoid that symbolized the presence of a temporal portal. As far as the Confederation was concerned, the newcomer was a skewline.

Skewlines were something I understood very well. A skewline is one that runs counter to the local flow in Paratime, a timeline with few if any connections to other universes.

Europo-American is a skewline. One of the reasons we had yet to discover crosstime travel was that we seldom have anyplace to go. Several of the experiments that lead to the development of time shuttles only show positive results in the presence of an active temporal portal. On my home line, the formation of portals is something that has happened infrequently over the last fifty thousand years. In fact, the last time a portal opened prior to the modern one, Athens and Sparta were slugging it out for dominance of the Peloponnesian Peninsula.

I couldn't help wondering how much ancient mythology was mere storytelling and how much investigative reporting.

"You think the Dalgir was from this hypothetical third line?" Haret asked.

"That is what we are going to find out."

"How?"

"We've plotted a sequence of temporal passages that should allow us to reach the line in question. Unfortunately, the last jump is from a line friendly to the Dalgiri Empire, so there is risk."

"Why tell us?" I asked. "More specifically, why tell me? I've only been training here for a little more than a year and a half. Surely you should have a crew of trained Watchmen."

Dal's face lit up with a smile reminiscent of the Mona Lisa. I wondered briefly if he had ever seen the painting and was doing it on purpose. "When I was given this assignment, Duncan, I thought immediately of you. You are my—" His expression went blank for an instant, as if he were consulting an overstuffed mental file. "—rabbit's foot. I believe that is the expression."

"Huh?"

"I was on duty in our control center in New York the night Jana Dougwaix reported that she had killed a Dalgir and had taken an outtimer into her confidence. And later, when she learned the Dalgiri objective, I was the first person she told. It was I who advised her to invite you to join the Watch. And again, when the Ruling Council was having doubts about your authenticity, I had a hand in convincing them to take a chance on you."

"You seem to be my guardian angel. Why?"

"Do you believe in fate?"

I shook my head.

"Neither do I, except where you are concerned. The fact that the Dalgiri dispatched an expedition into the past to kill you would seem to validate your destiny. Their attempt virtually guarantees that your life will be long and full. Now who would be better on a mission into the Empire? Besides, I was impressed by your people during my stay on Europo-American. You do not think as we do. It will be useful to have you along for your different viewpoint."

I had heard the "destined for greatness" argument before; and, frankly, I wasn't convinced. For one thing, I didn't *feel* like one of history's movers and shakers. Still, as I had muttered to myself several times in the past, I was in no position to argue. So I let discretion be my guide. I kept my mouth shut.

Dal turned to Haret. "As for the other member of our little team, I remember you as a bright student and your record on staff here at the Academy has been excellent. We're going to need a cultures specialist if that timeline is inhabited.

"Do either of you wish to decline to participate?"

I looked at Haret and she looked back at me. Neither of us said anything for a long time. Finally, I cleared my throat and turned to Dal Corst.

"When do we leave?"

It was to be a journey of six stages, a tortured path that crossed half a dozen timelines to reach the hypothetical Dalgiri base.

The first two transitions proved deceptively simple. Within half an hour of our arrival at the Academy shuttle port, we were at the Salfa Prime portal, making the jump to Salfa Null in an instant. Then it was a few hundred easy miles to the portal that would take us to the Association of Rivan City-States, one of the lesser timelines of the Confederation. After the Salfa Null–Riva transition, things began to drag a bit. Our next connection was half-way around the planet.

And I discovered a universal constant.

The shuttle was a standard Taladoran design, a fifteen-meter, ebon egg. As soon as we cleared the portal, Dal Corst lifted it high into the stratosphere and headed north over the Pole. Our next jump would take place in twelve hours over an ersatz Kansas prairie.

"Why so long?" I asked.

"Rivan regulation," Dal answered, throwing the words carelessly over his shoulder as he punched our course into the navigation computer. "We aren't allowed to exceed the speed of sound over land. The sonic shock would disturb the people living below."

From that point on I had a name for our blackened steed. Within the privacy of my own mind, she was *Concorde*.

Following Riva, we transitioned to a bleak, desert land-scape where hurricane winds scoured topsoil from the plains, blackening the sky. Ahead lay a ten-hour flight as we recrossed what should have been the Atlantic Ocean. This newest portal was different. All the others had been rock-steady. The latest portal, however, raced across the landscape before us in free flight. Dal chased an imaginary volume through the stratosphere for most of an hour, the shuttle's lift-and-drive generators screaming from the punishment, before the barren landscape was replaced by a lush rain forest of oddly yellow-green vegetation.

"Where are we?" I asked, peering at the screen in front of the pilot station.

"This timeline is identified only by its number." Dal then reeled off a string of figures longer than a Florida driver's license.

"Where should we set down?" Haret asked, her attention riveted on the detector readouts.

I counted the number of transitions we had gone through and came up with a total of five. That meant that the final jump was coming up. Unfortunately, the portal we would use for the final leg of our journey could have been labeled Old Faithless. It formed and dissolved on a maddeningly irregular schedule. It would be ten days before it opened again. There was no rushing Father Paratime, so we would have to sit down and await the inevitable.

"I would suggest a lake near the portal site."

Lakes are plentiful in rain forests, it seemed, so we had no difficulty finding a suitable candidate in which to hide the shuttle. We were in Dalgiri territory and had to keep under cover. After sinking the black shuttle beneath the dark blue waters of a deep mountain lake, we set up camp on the shore and began to enjoy our period of enforced relaxation. In the daytime we hiked, fished, swam, and basked in the sun. At night, we sat around a campfire in a nearby cave—its light well shielded from above—and talked.

No matter what subject we started with, before the evening was over the talk always came back to the same thing:

Paratime!

"I don't get it," I said on our next-to-last night in the cave.

"Don't get what?" Dal asked absently. His attention was focused more on the wild pig roasting over the fire than on me.

"Time portals. Why do they tend to form in one place and stay there?"

He scratched lazily and looked up. "Now I don't get you."

"Well, look." I grabbed a stick from our woodpile and began to draw in the dirt floor.

"Oh-oh," Haret said, "he's starting to scratch in the mud again."

We all laughed, but I continued to wield my stick. I didn't consider the evening complete until I had drawn at least one diagram to get my point across.

"Here's the Sun," I said, making a crude circle in the center of the cleared space. "It's going off—like so—as it revolves around the center of mass of the Galaxy. Now here we are on the Earth . . ." I used the Temporal Basic word which, of course, meant exactly the same thing. ". . . and it's revolving around the Sun. Now, to complicate matters further, the Earth is revolving on its own axis, meaning that we are speeding along at about a thousand miles an hour on top of everything else. You with me so far?"

They nodded.

"So how can time gates be fixed in space with respect to this whirling dervish?"

Dal sat back on his haunches and looked at me with serious eyes. "If I remember, Duncan, your people have developed the theory that space is stretched in the region of large masses, have they not?"

"Curved," I said, nodding. "That's one of Einstein's theories."

"Curved, then. Can you not see that it is this curvature that is one of the prime components of the conditions that cause a temporal portal to form in the first place?"

"No."

"It's a matter of energy. In theory, we could jump any size temporal barrier if we just had sufficient energy available to us. Of course, generally we don't and are thus severely restricted in our movements.

"All forms of energy—potential, kinetic, entropic, temporal—are conserved in a Paratime jump. That is a basic law of the universe. The portals are just places where the energy level between universes almost matches. We make up for any difference.

"Now, occasionally, you get a portal much like the one we just came through. Such a region is the result of an instability between the two congruent universes. The region is always on the verge of disappearing and reappearing somewhere else. After a few years of existence, the precarious balance will tip one way or the other and the two timelines will diverge from each other.

"Is it not obvious that the necessity for equal gravitational potential on both sides of the portal causes that portal to share the Earth's rotation? Are not the lines of constant spatial curvature, in effect, spinning in harmony with the mass that creates the curvature in the first place?"

I looked at the diagram I had drawn, and shrugged. It wasn't obvious to me, but I would take his word for it. He was the expert.

Dal grinned like the canary who had swallowed the cat.

"What's the matter?" I asked.

"I've been wondering if I made the right choice of personnel for this mission. You have just confirmed my original opinion."

"Huh?"

"Not one Taladoran in a thousand understands what *you* have just explained. We Paratimers still think of the Earth as the center of the universe because, to us, it truly is. Your people, with no place to go but out into space, have a much clearer world view than we. Beyond the atmosphere, you are the sophisticates and we the primitives. Your insights and observations on this trip may prove invaluable."

"Just call me Copernicus," I said, matching him grin for grin.

His expression changed to one of puzzlement. "Who?"

Forty-eight hours later we were once again aloft. Dal sat rigidly at the controls, scanning the screen in front of him, while Haret bent over her instruments. I tried to stay out of the way while watching everything at once.

Somewhere in front of us two universes were slowly drifting toward congruency.

"Fifty centibora," Haret announced.

Another eight minutes and we would be through. Anticipation mounted in *Concorde*'s cabin.

Outside, it was early morning. Ten miles below, a yellow-green rain forest stretched to the horizon and a thousand patches of water glowed with reflected fire as the sun climbed the eastern sky. Of the soon-to-be-formed portal, there was no sight—but, of course, there wouldn't be.

"Transtemporal field," Dal called. A low hum was added to the gentle whisper of the lift-and-drive generators. The transition generators had begun to accumulate the charge that would soon drive us to another world.

The sound reminded me of the topic of discussion for our last night in the cave.

"I just don't see it," I had said, once more seated with drawing stick in hand. "If there can be congruency between separate universes, why not between two points in the same universe?"

"What would be the use?" Haret had asked. "You would be in the same universe you started in."

"But in a different spot! It would be practical teleportation. No more ten-hour jaunts between portals. Every point on the planet would be no more than an instant away."

Dal Corst looked thoughtful. "I never thought of it that way," he said, scratching at a week-old growth of beard. Our ten days in the sun had caused us to go a bit native and none of us was looking forward to returning to the quest on the morrow. "I can't be sure until I look at the mathematics, of course. Seems to me that the equations don't allow a ship to reappear in the same gravitational field it started in."

"Twenty centibora," Haret said, snapping me back to the present. "The portal is taking shape nicely."

"Stand ready for transtemporal transition," Dal sang out.

Concorde began to slide forward toward the invisible gate between worlds, gathering speed by the second.

The normal procedure for passing through a time gate

is to hover within the volume of space that defines the portal and trigger the transition generators in an instantaneous burst of fifth-dimensional lightning. There are good, practical reasons for getting rid of all forward velocity prior to the jump between universes. If the energies of transition are not precisely balanced, the offending shuttle can go up in a convincing replica of an H-Bomb explosion.

But hovering within a portal is a good way to get your ass shot off on the other side.

Since we had no way of knowing who—or what—was waiting for us, we were using a riskier procedure. Dal drove *Concorde* forward at full power, accelerating until we were traveling at nearly Mach 3. Then, in the seconds after the portal formed, we would dive through the hundred-meter-diameter, irregular volume that was the congruency and trigger our generators. If everything went well, we would pop out into a new world like an avenging angel, and be over the horizon before the hypothetical portal defenders could react.

If it didn't, if the generators discharged a millisecond too early or too late . . .

"Coming up on the portal," Dal screamed above the moan of the lift-and-drive. "Hold tight, we're going through!"

The green plain continued to slip beneath us while the deep purple sky remained unchanged. Suddenly *Concorde* lurched as if in turbulence, and the world below turned white. A blanket of clouds covered the Earth from horizon to horizon, and early morning turned suddenly into high noon.

Dal turned to Haret, his face split by a wide grin. He opened his mouth to speak—

—and the world exploded in a blaze of violet light around us.

CHAPTER 7

I woke to the sound of coughing and opened my eyes to a darkened universe turned topsy-turvy. The coughing came again and I realized that it was coming from me. After the spasm passed, I looked around.

Concorde lay on her back. Dal, Haret, and I hung from the ceiling like slabs of prime beef, held in place by our safety harnesses. I peered forward through the gloom. Nothing could be seen except the dim outlines of my teammates' heads and arms hanging limply below the deeper shadows that marked the seatbacks.

I groaned and reached up to unsnap my harness.

The next thing I knew I was in free-fall. I barely managed to get my arms below me to cushion the impact as I slammed into the hard overhead below me.

I lay where I fell, taking inventory of my situation. Those few seconds after transition were a jumble. First there was that flash of eye-searing violet, and then . . . what?

I remembered that as Dal fought his crippled craft, he used a few words of Basic that the teaching machines hadn't taught me. Most four-letter words in Temporal Basic have at least three syllables.

Haret's voice had been remarkably calm throughout those few moments after the explosion. I remembered her reading from the emergency checklist even as we plummeted toward the blanket of clouds below.

"What happened?" I had half-asked, half-screamed.

"Fixed battery," Dal said. "We were unlucky. Now shut up and let me get this monster under control."

He struggled for an eternity that lasted no more than

thirty seconds before throwing up his hands in disgust and mouthing another short, pungent comment. This one he could only have heard on the streets of New York City.

"Hopeless," he said, reaching out for the control panel. "Hang on, I'm going to jettison."

A giant fist slammed into my spine before his words stopped echoing through the cabin. After that, there was only darkness for an interminable time until my own hacking cough woke me.

I gathered what strength I had left and hoisted myself to a sitting position. Nothing appeared to be broken. At least no excruciating jab of pain greeted my experiments.

I crawled to where Haret and Dal hung from the ceiling like two flies caught in a spiderweb. Haret moaned as I unstrapped and gently lowered her to the overhead-cum-deck beneath us. She stirred, and peered upward into the gloom.

"Duncan, are you all right?"

I nodded then reassured her with a few words and turned to Dal. He was a lot heavier than Haret and a much more awkward burden as I lowered him. His limp body got away from me and the next thing I knew, I was gasping for breath under his body.

"How is he?" Haret asked after I had squirmed out from under.

"Alive," I said, leaning over to place my ear against his chest. "Not responding, though. I need light."

There was a soft scrabbling sound from the rear of the cabin and lights blazed beneath us. The sudden brightness hurt my eyes.

In the light, Dal didn't look too bad. I ran my hands over him, checking for broken bones. I could find none, but there was a nasty gash on his head, just above the hairline. I brought my hand away covered with blood. "Possible concussion. How about you, Haret? Are you hurt?"

She shrugged. "Apparently not. Where are we, Duncan?"

"Good question." I moved to the rear hatch, the one that used to lead to the staterooms and the engine compartment. Upon opening it, I discovered a forest panorama of dark green trees and underbrush, and a leaden sky. A slow drizzle fell from the solid bank of clouds overhead.

I glanced at Haret over my shoulder. She was making Dal more comfortable. "I'm going to look around a bit."

"Don't get lost, Duncan." In spite of the forced calm of her voice, I could sense her fear of being left alone on a strange world with an unconscious companion.

"I won't."

I stepped from the security of the flight cabin to the cold drizzle outside, shivering slightly as I did so.

Concorde had come to rest on the side of a hill. Or rather, *Concorde*'s emergency capsule had. What had once been the flight cabin lay majestically in a bower of ruined pinelike trees and deep brush, its cable-encrusted belly pointed toward the sky. The exterior of the cabin showed signs of scorching, as if someone had taken a giant blowtorch to it. Of the rest of the ship, there was no sign.

I walked carefully around the capsule, scanning the area for signs of civilization. There were none. I hiked to the top of the ridge above the ship and scouted out a large outcrop of rock from which to survey the countryside. Forest green extended all the way to the horizon. To my right, a tree-covered mountain disappeared into the gray blanket of clouds. To the left, endless rolling hills like the one I was on marched into the distance.

Nowhere in my line of sight was there any sign of man.

My shoulders shuddered involuntarily as I pulled my tunic collar more tightly around me. For all I knew, we were marooned on an uninhabited timeline with no hope of rescue. I ruthlessly put that morbid thought from my mind. Even Dalgiri would be preferable to endless wilderness. With them, at least, we would have a way home if we were clever enough to seize the opportunity.

Besides, *Concorde* had been blasted from the sky. What could be more civilized than a gun programmed to shoot down strangers the instant they appeared?

Back inside the cabin, I closed the hatch and returned to Haret's side. She sat cross-legged on the overhead with Dal's head in her lap as she bandaged it.

"Any change?"

"No. He sleeps peacefully—too peacefully. We can only pray that he comes out of it on his own. What did you find outside?"

I reviewed what I had seen. Haret listened intently. I finished all too quickly with: "It's too bad about the clouds. We might have been able to see signs of civilization on the way in if it weren't so goddamned overcast."

"And those who shot us down could have seen us as well. Be thankful for the weather. It has probably saved our lives—for a while, at least."

"Where's the weapons locker?"

"Through the door behind you, second bin on the right," she said, gesturing with her eyes.

I straightened up from my crouch, and stopped in mid-movement. I had already been through the door behind me. Only forest lay on the other side. I sat back down, letting myself drop heavily to the overhead.

"The weapons were in the back of the ship?"

"I'm afraid so."

I repeated the short, pungent English word Dal had used earlier. Somehow it made me feel better.

We spent the rest of the daylight hours inventorying our supplies. The tally was disheartening. We had no food, no water, no weapons. By dark, even our lighting system was starting to show the strain. We switched off the lights to save the power packs. I clutched a pair of light-amplifying glasses in case we received visitors during the night while Haret slept in my arms.

Over the next three days we set up housekeeping in a clearing a quarter mile downhill from the wreck. We built a crude lean-to next to a small creek, and I snared a few rabbits to eat. Haret tended Dal and a small campfire.

By the end of the third day we had settled into a routine of sorts.

"I've been thinking about rabbits," I said while skinning a big jack.

"What about rabbits?" Haret asked as she roasted another small carcass marshmallow-style over the fire.

"Why rabbits? Why not little furry dinosaurs, or walking jellyfish, or birds with teeth?"

"I don't understand."

"The various universes of Paratime have been separate

since the Big Bang, right? So why all the similar fauna and flora? They should have developed as independent timelines, with no common heritage at all. Just because my line grew people with two arms, two legs, and a head, why should all the other timelines copy us so closely?"

She hesitated a moment before answering: "No one knows for sure."

"Huh?"

"Oh, there are theories, of course. Most think there is a natural cross-pollination between timelines. There appear to be cases when the temporal barriers break down and animals—or human beings—accidentally cross from one universe to another. Nobody has yet come up with a mechanism that explains how such a thing could happen, but that is the theory."

I thought about it. It made sense. Weren't people at home always disappearing mysteriously? Why not Mother Nature's own version of a transtemporal shuttle? It was certainly more believable than a billion cases of convergent evolution.

"Sounds like a good subject for a doctoral thesis," I said.

"It has been—thousands of times. One branch of biology studies nothing else. You can trace a timeline's history by looking at the relationship of its living things to the universes around it. The longer two lines are in contact, the more alike their evolutionary histories. After a billion years or so of intimate contact with each other, some of the core universes of the interdependent clusters are virtually indistinguishable from one another. In other universes, especially the skewlines, diversity is the norm."

I nodded. I had already discovered that Talador and Salfa Prime were relatively tame by comparison to what I was used to back home. Snakes were unknown on both timelines, for instance. Not for the first time, I wondered whether the Garden of Eden fable might not have a basis in fact.

I was jolted from my reverie by a sharp intake of breath from Haret. "What's the matter?"

It took her a moment to find her voice. When she did, she spoke in a husky whisper: "Behind you, four men sneaking up on us. I don't think they realize I've spotted them."

My mind raced for a few seconds as my eyes darted all around, seeking a way out. I thought up a dozen daring escapes in as many seconds, discarding each as quickly. The sharp snap of a twig breaking underfoot echoed through the clearing and I did the most intelligent thing I could think of.

I stood slowly, keeping my hands well away from my sides, and turned around—smiling.

They were all seven-foot-tall, red-bearded conquistadors.

At least that was my first impression. It didn't last long. On second glance I realized that their armor was nothing like that of sixteenth-century Spain. Only the peaked helmets were similar. Otherwise, they wore leather cuirasses something like those of the Romans, and green jackboots. Each man had a long sword strung across his back, presumably secured in place by the Sam Browne belt that draped from left to right across his chest. At their belts, two of them wore heavy-handled daggers, almost trench knives with full, knuckle-duster grips.

But what interested me most were the muskets they held in their hands. I found myself staring down four gaping, black muzzles. The stocks, which I couldn't see very well because of foreshortening, looked more Afghan than Western. The firing mechanism was a cross between wheel lock and flintlock. The overall impression, however, was of deadly efficiency.

I smiled and raised my arms with palms upright in front of me. "Friend," I felt silly as I said it.

A man with slightly more ornate leatherwear than the others' opened his mouth and spoke a short sentence. The words were gibberish, but whatever they meant, they bore the sting of command.

"What do you think?" I asked Haret over my shoulder.

The order came again, this time accompanied by a sharp gesture from a musket barrel.

"He wants us to move away from Dal, I think."

That was the way I had read it. "Exit stage right or get

your head busted," seemed to be the gist of the conversation so far. We backed off a few paces.

Another sharp command split the cool air and the number-four man lowered his weapon and crossed the clearing until he stood over Dal. We had been pouring broth of rabbit down Dal for two days and he had instinctively swallowed, but otherwise showed no signs of waking. The native leaned down and expertly ran his fingers through Dal's hair. He quickly found the dent in the Watchman's skull.

A quick conference of barks suddenly ended in more orders. Before I realized what was happening, rough hands grabbed me by the arms and bent until my wrists were crossed behind me. I stood still while a rawhide strap was fastened around them. When I was securely bound, my two captors crossed to Haret and repeated the performance.

The conquistadors turned their attention once more to Dal. I got the impression the two younger captors—teenagers with scraggly beards and bad acne—wanted to kill Dal to save the trouble of transporting him. The third underling, the one who had played Doctor, seemed indifferent. However, the Leader was obviously loath to lose even one captive and, after a few minutes' argument, had his three companions cut wood for a stretcher while he leaned on the barrel of his gun and eyed us warily.

Within a half-hour the party was moving through thick forest, following the small creek downstream. The Leader walked at the head of the column, followed by us, followed by the sharp-eyed Doctor as guard. The two juvenile delinquents brought up the rear, grumbling. Carrying the stretcher had fallen to them.

Where the creek ran into a small river, we found four shaggy horses tethered to a line run between two trees. There were more discussions, concerning the rigging of a horse litter, and a brief rest while the litter was being constructed. Then, suddenly, we were off again. This time, however, the Leader and the Doctor rode while Haret and I stumbled along behind. The other two took turns riding the spare horse while the loser led the horse with the stretcher.

We walked for the rest of the day, always moving

downstream, stopping only when it was too dark to see the river rock and broken branches underfoot. Haret and I spent a fitful night huddled together, trussed up like a couple of prize pigs. Then it was up at dawn, a light breakfast of leathery dried meat, and off again.

It wasn't until midday that we finally left the forest and entered a wide clearing of knee-high brush and wild flowers. By this time the stream had grown to a respectable river. I sank gratefully to my knees as the leader called a momentary halt. I looked up.

In the distance, sitting atop a hill, was a castle right out of a Hollywood swashbuckler.

The Leader turned in his saddle and followed my gaze.

"Fyalsorn," he said, pointing.

CHAPTER 8

It took another six hours of walking to reach the gates of the city that surrounded the hilltop castle. It was a walled town of narrow, winding streets where the buildings tended to squeeze out the little sunlight that made it through the clouds.

We trudged through the gloom along crowded thoroughfares with all of the stinks of any oriental bazaar. My nose quickly told me that the locals ate beef, had a knowledge of spices ranging from mint to cloves, and grew a particularly offensive variety of tobacco. Overpowering all of these olfactory stimulants, however, was the smell that emanated from the dirty little stream that flowed down the center of every street.

"What do you think of the local color, Haret?" She was stumbling along beside me. I could tell by her expression that the rawhide straps chafed her as badly as they did me.

She smiled grimly. "I believe I understand the reference," she said, wrinkling her nose, "and it isn't the color that bothers me."

We reached the gate of the castle by full dark. I was panting from the exertion by the time we reached the top of the bluff overlooking the town. Even so, I stared. Castles are out of style in the world I come from.

Fyalsorn—if that was the name of the castle and not the town—was obviously intended to be a working fortress. A solid edifice built of sandstone blocks and complete with battlements, turrets, and towers, not one of those fairyland showplaces much favored by mad kings of Bavaria and others. We crossed a drawbridge that spanned a hand-hewn chasm and entered the courtyard just inside the gate. It was there that I got my first surprise.

I had pegged our hosts at sixteenth- or seventeenth-century Europe. But sitting to one side of the courtyard, puffing and billowing black smoke from a tall sandstone chimney, was a coal-fired, walking-beam steam engine. That was the least of the surprise, however. The armorers of the fourteenth century could have built a simple steam engine if they'd known how. The technology for placing a man inside a removable covering of plate iron light enough to allow him to sit a horse was every bit as complex as boilermaking. But our captors had gone far beyond mere steam. Attached to the engine was a crude electric generator. There was no doubt about the nature of the big wheel because the interior of the courtyard was illuminated by the harsh glare of carbon-arc lamps mounted high on the surrounding wall.

"A fairly advanced timeline," Haret said, looking around. "We should be able to deal with them."

I nodded. "If they don't sell us to the Dalgiri first."

The three riders dismounted and let castle guards take their mounts. Other guards unstrapped the horse litter from the fourth animal and it too was taken away. Haret and I were ushered up a flight of stairs into a great hall lit by hissing lamps.

Haret stared around her, drinking in every detail. "Why not use electric light inside?"

I shrugged. "Arc lights are too powerful, I guess. I would bet that those mantel lanterns burn hydrogen, though. That means either coal gas or electrolysis."

At a barked command from the Leader, we stopped in the middle of the great hall while two castle guards cut our bonds. Within seconds fire coursed through my hands as blood began flowing once more.

When the worst of the burning had become merely pins and needles, we were ushered through a doorway and up a long spiral staircase that ended at a stout locked door. One of the guards inserted a great iron key into the huge padlock—you could insert two fingers into the keyhole—and turned it. The door swung out on silent hinges as our party clumped inside. The Leader used a tinderbox to light a candle, then pointed out the various refinements in the room: a straw mattress with canvas ticking, a scratchy blanket, a rough-hewn table on which the candle and an earthen pitcher sat, and an oak bucket filled with water. I puzzled over the latter until I realized that it must be the sanitary facilities.

Our guards stomped out in their mud-covered boots and the Leader paused to say something before exiting through the door and closing it behind him. A brief clank sounded as the lock was turned, then we could hear footsteps retreating down the staircase.

I crossed to the door and listened for other sounds. Before long I heard the scrape of metal against stone. They had posted a guard.

I straightened up and gave Haret the news.

"Did you expect any different?"

I shrugged.

"What do you think the officer said just before he left?" she asked.

"Could have been anything from 'Have a nice sleep' to 'Welcome to the tower of London.' "

"Welcome to what?"

"Never mind."

"What about Dal? Do you think they'll harm him?"

"Why carry him all that way and kill him here? They probably took him to their hospital, assuming, of course, that they have one."

"So what do we do?" Haret asked, looking around the bare room. The wind outside moaned and rain pattered against the stained-glass window opposite the bed.

"Get a good night's sleep. What else can we do?"

We slipped out of our dirty gray jumpsuits and crawled beneath the equally dirty gray blanket. I reached out and snuffed the candle flame between thumb and forefinger. Haret was a spot of silken warmth in an otherwise prickly and cold universe as we held each other close. We lay there in silence until her shoulders began to shake with quiet sobs.

"What's the matter?" I whispered.

As if my speaking were the cue, a soft mewling sound emanated from her throat and tears flowed freely as she buried her face in the cradle formed by my upper arm and chest. I held her close. Eventually the sobs subsided.

"Better?" I asked.

"I'm frightened, Duncan. What if they *are* clients of the Dalgiri?"

"Let's just see how things develop. In the meantime..."

I searched for her lips in the darkness and quickly found them. An unknown time later I found myself caressing taut nipples and being caressed in return. Then, as if driven by demons, we moved on to greater intimacies. It was well past midnight when we drifted to sleep, our bodies still entwined.

Language lessons began the next morning after a breakfast of what could only have been porridge. Our teacher was a stooped old warrior with arthritis so bad he could barely walk. His name was Argor, and he quickly gave evidence of possessing a first-class mind. Like everyone else we had seen, he was a redhead, although his mane was diminished by a large bald spot and a generous wreath of gray hair.

After a week of dawn-to-dusk sessions, Haret and I had a smattering of the local language. Perhaps it was the Watch's training program or just the fact that I had recently had to learn a dozen new languages. Whatever the cause, I found I could pick up new words almost as quickly as I heard them.

The language was called Swajorn, the castle was indeed Fyalsorn, and the town which we could open our window and gaze down upon was Fyalsorn-Daya—literally, the city under the protection of Fyalsorn Castle. The master of the castle was Lord Ryfik, whose son, Lord Gosfik, had been the leader of the party that found us.

As soon as we had the vocabulary, we asked Argor about Dal.

He looked at us with rheumy blue eyes and said something I almost understood. After fifteen minutes of hard work on both sides, we concluded that Dal was under the care of the castle Chirurgeon. I quizzed Argor for several minutes before settling on "Chirurgeon" as the translation. Somehow Argor's description of a local physician just didn't fit my understanding of "doctor."

By the end of our second week of captivity, we were almost carrying on real conversations.

"How long are you going to hold us here, Argor?" I asked after lunch one day. The meal had consisted of a loaf of unleavened bread and a generous helping of roast beef well carbonized.

"That is for Lord Ryfik to decide, Honorables."

It seemed that both Haret and I were "honorables"—I the male form of the term, Haret the female. No one would tell us why. Whatever the reason, it probably accounted for the fact that our quarters were in the tower and not in the castle dungeon. I had already pried the information out of the guards that they had one.

"What of our friend?" Haret asked. "You have told us nothing since he regained his senses three days . . . uh, begone."

"Your friend has a hearty appetite and gains strength each night. Before long, he will join you here—that is, if you have no objection, Honorable."

"We do not object, Argor."

Three days later Lord Ryfik summoned us before him. The Fyalsorn Council Hall was big and empty; it reminded me of a church on Tuesday morning. There were row after row of pewlike seats where the faithful could sit and listen to the rulings of their Laird. A half-dozen flying buttresses swooped overhead, adding greatly to the impression that the room was more cathedral than hall of state. Stained-glass skylights far overhead reinforced the image.

Ryfik himself was as impressive as the room. He was a tall man with muted red hair. Specks of gray colored his temples and a scar ran diagonally across his right cheek. His complexion was a darker version of the red-cheeked, peaches-and-cream hue that appeared to be the local norm. He was conspicuous for his lack of a beard.

Haret and I marched down the aisle of the Council Hall and stopped a dozen paces from the throne as we had been instructed. Argor had said nothing about bowing or curtseying or any of the other silly things monarchs dream up for their underlings, so we just stood in what I hoped was a respectful posture.

Ryfik briefly looked over our grimy jumpsuits then signaled to one of the many well-armed guards standing inconspicuously in the shadows along the side of the hall. The man left through a side door and quickly returned holding an unsteady Dal Corst by one arm. The guard helped him to the center of the hall where we were standing.

Haret and I surrounded Dal as soon as the guard let him go. Haret kissed him and I pounded him on the back. He seemed disoriented for a moment, but somehow he gave the impression of being made of high-alloy steel in spite of his sunken cheeks and gaunt face.

"Report, Watchman. What is going on here?"

I sketched what had occurred since we transitioned the portal, then Haret filled in some of the gaps I had left. Ryfik watched with interest for about two minutes and then noisily cleared his throat.

The three of us stopped and faced the throne.

Court was obviously in session.

"We have waited long for a chance to take some of your people hostage, Honorables. What say you concerning a ransom? Will your king pay it?"

Ryfik's voice boomed out over the empty hall, so much so that I suspected the palace architect must have had at least a working knowledge of acoustics. He spoke slowly and clearly, enunciating more carefully than was normal in Swajorn. Even so, I had to mull his words over a bit before I could attach meaning to them. I suddenly realized what was wrong as I listened to Haret whisper a quick translation to Dal.

These people had mistaken us for the Dalgiri!

"You are wrong, Lord," I boomed out in my best imitation of Ryfik's baritone. "Those from whom you would extort our ransom are our sworn enemies."

The echo had barely died in the great hall when I realized that I might have found a more tactful way of expressing myself. I turned to Dal, who continued to stare ahead, his expression determined.

"You have it, Watchman," he whispered out of the side of his mouth. "For all of our sakes, make it good."

Ryfik, for his part, merely narrowed a bit further the slits that were his eyes. "What say you?"

"Those who have wronged you are called Dalgiri. We are of Talador and are their sworn enemies."

This set off an excited buzzing among the courtiers that quickly died under Ryfik's withering glance.

"Explain, Honorable!"

I gave him a sanitized rundown of the Taladoran Confederation's war with the Dalgiri Empire, carefully avoiding any explanation of where we all came from. I was willing to bet that these people had explored their own Earth well enough to know that we and the Dalgiri were from somewhere else. I hoped they had no inkling of exactly where that somewhere else really was.

When I finished, Ryfik leaned back and regarded me suspiciously. "What say you, son?"

Gosfik looked us over and shrugged. "They are not exactly the same as the others, that is true. But how to be sure they are not of the others? Perhaps we deal with two separate clans of the same kingdom."

"What say you, Honorable?"

"What can I say? If you believe us, perhaps we can help you against the Dalgiri. If not, then you are no closer to throwing off their yoke than before."

"True." Ryfik sat deep in thought.

Haret took advantage of the pause to whisper in my ear. "Ask about the Dalgiri. What have those monsters done?"

"How has my enemy wronged you, Lord?"

The tale was long, but, basically, the Dalgiri just appeared one day and began to build a stronghold in a valley fifty miles from the castle. Their base was a cluster of silver domes—Dal thought a research station when Haret described it to him—surrounded by an electric fence and defended by automatic beamers.

If the Dalgiri's activities were strange to Ryfik, they were all too familiar to Dal, Haret, and me. The Empire's methods were time-honored and very effective. First its agents learned the local language and culture by kidnaping victims and probing their minds with computer-operated psych machines. Since the interviewees were damaged irretrievably in the process, the Dalgiri normally killed them afterward.

And that wasn't the worst of it.

Ryfik had quickly organized a raiding party to show the strangers the folly of trespassing on Fyalsorn territory. Luckily, the team hadn't been large—twenty or so castle guards under the command of Ryfik's wife's uncle. None of the raiders had returned, although a couple of horses had wandered home after a month or so.

And soon the Dalgiri had taken to raids of their own. Outlying villages were set upon by shuttles two or three times a year to teach the locals a continuing lesson. Ryfik's ministers thought the captives were being held hostage in the Dalgiri station, insurance against Fyalsorn's good behavior—a logical conclusion since just such a system was standard statecraft locally.

At story's end, I held a hurried, whispered conference with Dal and Haret. "What do you think? Do we tell them the hostages are all dead or would rather be?"

Dal bit his lip in indecision. "That might drive him over to our side, or it might throw him into a rage. You know what happens to the bearer of bad news."

"Haret?"

"No opinion, Duncan."

"We've got to tell them something. See the way the Lord is squirming up there?"

"The truth then," Dal said. "It has been known to work on occasion."

So I told them. I explained graphically the psych-probe process, emphasizing the condition of the probee afterward. As I spoke, searching my limited supply of Swajorn words for the right ones, a hush fell over the assembly. Ryfik's expression, which had been merely interested, took on a dark scowl. When I had finished my little horror story, his rage was obvious. I noticed more than one hand in the crowd reaching for a weapon. The silence was suddenly interrupted by a single voice slowly sobbing. I realized the source was one of the guards who lined the hall.

Ryfik spoke finally, enunciating each word slowly and with emphasis, spitting them out as if they tasted bad.

"Is . . . this . . . true?"

"I swear it, Lord."

"We shall see. If it is, I shall wage holy war against these demons. If not . . ."

I nodded. If Ryfik found I was lying, the three "honor-ables" from distant Talador would find themselves guests of Fyalsorn's dungeonmaster.

I could feel the hot splints under my fingernails already.

CHAPTER 9

A few quick words from Ryfik and the public audience was over. Four of the most capable-looking guards convoyed Dal, Haret, and me to the Lord's private quarters. There, clustered around a small chart table before a cozy fire, were Ryfik, Gosfik, our mentor Argor, and two worthies I tentatively dubbed "Secretary of State" and "Commanding General."

As the three of us took our places opposite Ryfik, he looked up from the parchment map before him. His anger had cooled a bit, and an air of calculation had taken its place.

"Now, Honorables, if what you say is true, there will be war. How do we verify your story?"

Proving ourselves to Ryfik turned out to be a major undertaking. Haret and I took turns describing our distant "country," and what had happened from the moment we were shot down until Gosfik captured us. We answered questions for three hours, but we always returned to the same point.

How to prove that we spoke the truth?

Finally, Argor looked up from where he warmed his aching bones before the fire and suggested a plan.

"This flying machine is near where young Gos found you?"

"Yes," I said.

Argor cleared his throat in a deep growl and turned to Ryfik. "Then, Lord, we have a means of testing the Honorable's truthfulness. Our fight with the invaders has not been totally without plunder. We have samples of the chicken scratching they use in place of honest Swajorn lettering. Surely if these three are of another kingdom, their language will be different from that of the stooped ones."

I translated Argor's idea for Dal, who immediately agreed. "Of course! Why didn't I think of it? Dalgiri script is so different from Taladoran that even a blind man could see the difference."

I nodded. Dalgiri writing was reminiscent of Morse code—all dots and dashes—while Taladoran bore a striking resemblance to the script in a Gutenberg Bible crossed with Arabic.

"Where do we find a sample of Taladoran script?" Haret asked.

"That's why Argor asked about the ship," I said. "We take them to the emergency capsule, show them the lettering on our instruments, and they believe us—I hope."

The rest of the afternoon was taken up with the negotiations as to who would accompany the Fyalsornan party to the wreckage of our ship. A bargain was finally struck, one that I wasn't particularly happy with—Dal and I would accompany Lord Ryfik, his son, and a heavily armed party back; Haret would remain behind as a hostage.

We started at dawn the next morning. For the first time since our arrival on the Fyalsornan timeline, patches of blue sky were visible. The party was nearly fifty strong counting our guards. When pack animals and spare horses were included, we made an impressive procession.

Dal and I rode behind the nobles while two sharp-eyed warriors rode behind us, their weapons conspicuously loosened in their holsters. They made no attempt to keep us from conversing in Temporal Basic. Their sole duty was to prevent an escape.

"I want to compliment you on the way you handled the old fire breather yesterday," Dal said as we picked our way along the river bank. He looked strangely at home in the leather outfit Ryfik had supplied each of us.

"I had to do something, Dal. I'm certainly not much of a good-luck charm on this trip."

"Nonsense. We're alive, aren't we?"

"Not because of me. When I think of all the millions

of others Jana Dougwaix could have contacted, people who can handle themselves in an emergency . . ."

Dal grinned. "We may ask you for a list of candidates sooner than you think."

"I don't understand."

Dal hesitated for a moment, as if considering whether or not to let me in on a confidence. "It's not for public consumption, but the Council has been watching your performance very carefully. There is considerable sentiment for inviting Europo-American to join the Confederation."

"There is?" The news wasn't as welcome as I had expected it to be. I couldn't quite identify the reason for my dismay. I didn't dislike the Taladorans. By most standards they were good people. But they weren't *my* people, and I guess that was it. The idea of the Confederation overpowering my home timeline bothered me. Oh, not that they would conquer us or anything like that. Experience had shown them the futility of trying to hold a timeline against its will. But culturally, Talador would do to Western Civilization what we Westerners had done to so many others. We would be annexed and overwhelmed. As provincial as Europo-American was, it seemed to me that we had something unique. I wouldn't be happy to see it destroyed—even by someone who meant us well.

"Most of the opposition in Council centers on the fact that Europo-American isn't part of our transtemporal cluster," Dal said. "If we discover the Dalgiri process for doing without portals, that won't matter anymore. All of Paratime will be open to us."

The conversation quieted after that. We had entered deep forest and it was too difficult to talk while riding single file along the deer trails. It gave me a lot of time to think.

It was early afternoon when our outriders galloped back to tell us that they had spotted our camp in the forest clearing. I could feel the adrenaline coursing through my veins as I spurred my horse into a gallop toward the wrecked escape module.

Concorde's broken cabin was where we had left it. Our troop of cavalrymen fanned out through deep brush as

Lork Ryfik, Gosfik, Dal, and I dismounted to search the wreckage.

I led the way through the rear hatchway, showing Ryfik everything with Taladoran script on it. His eyes captured every detail, searching for a slip that would prove I was lying. Finally, after fifteen minutes of probing and questioning, he grinned and took my hand in the backward grip that the Lords of Fyalsorn had used to seal their bargains for two hundred years.

"Welcome, friend," he said with tears in his eyes.

"May we fight well together," I said, doing my best to render my words in the same formal Swajorn that Ryfik had used. I then clasped arms with Gosfik while Dal did the same with Ryfik.

When oaths of fealty had been exchanged all around, Ryfik turned to me. "Let us depart this coffin, Honorable. My back will curve like Argor's should I delay a moment longer."

Ryfik, Gosfik, and I climbed down from the emergency pod while Dal began pulling circuit modules from their holders. "Be out in a minute," he said. "These will be of use later."

I translated for Ryfik.

I had to give him this much: if he suspected that Dal might be rummaging around in there for a weapon he never gave the slightest clue. Apparently, on this timeline a man's sworn word meant something.

Or maybe Ryfik just didn't have time to think through all the implications. As we emerged back into the sunlight, the quiet of the surrounding forest was disturbed by the simultaneous explosion of a dozen muskets.

Once I would have stared transfixed in the direction of the firing. No longer. As the gunshots echoed through the hills and I dove for cover, I saw a silent lightning flash on the crest above *Concorde*, a flash that could only have come from a beamer.

And the only beamers on this timeline belonged to the Dalgiri.

There was considerable yelling and screaming from the perimeter as our guard force charged the area of battle. The firing began to pick up as more of them engaged the unseen foe. Twice, tree trunks exploded in geysers of superheated steam as beamer bolts struck them. And each time the firing returned a bit faster afterward. Lord Ryfik's men seemed fearless in the face of what to them must have been a terror weapon.

After several minutes of staccato firing, the woods were suddenly quiet once more. I lay where I was, my nose buried in a not-unpleasant-smelling carpet of damp pine needles, trying to see around a 360-degree circle without lifting my head. There was the noisy rustle of shrubbery from the direction of the battle, then a burly noncom burst into view.

"What is it, Zoor?" Ryfik asked.

The guard bent over, resting hands on knees, as he panted from the exertion. "The . . . invaders . . . Lord. They were watching . . . Wrof and Birst stumbled on them . . . Wrof is dead. Birst won't see the sunset. I think we wounded one."

"Where are they now?" I asked, trying to keep the panic from my voice.

The guard looked at me, dubious. Ryfik ordered him to answer.

"They had a flying wagon and made good their escape."

"Aircar," I muttered to myself in English. "They probably went back for reinforcements."

"I don't think so," a voice behind me said in Temporal Basic. Dal stood in the open hatchway of the escape module.

"What did the Honorable say?" Ryfik asked.

I told him and then turned back to Dal.

"If they found the wreckage, they must have found our camp and concluded that the locals had captured us. That means the two or three guards they left here were only to keep the locals away.

"A much larger force would undoubtedly be dispatched to search for us. And the first place I'd look if I were the Dalgiri would be—"

"—Fyalsorn Castle!" I yelped.

Dal agreed.

The news hit Ryfik like a sledgehammer when I translated for him. He uttered two words that were obviously oaths and began to yell orders in a tone that brought instant obedience. Within seconds the forest was alive with running horses and men as our troop began to assemble for the march home.

When they had gathered around, Ryfik mounted up and described the situation briefly. A low mutter rumbled through the ranks and there was much fingering of weaponry. "Home, lads," he concluded, wheeling his horse back the way we had come. "Fyalsorn is in mortal danger."

"Stop him," Dal yelled. "We need to strip the ship for parts. If we are going to attack a Dalgiri research station, we'll have to construct some modern weaponry."

I explained our need to Ryfik. I could sense his inner turmoil as he ordered ten guards and as many pack mules to stay behind with Dal. In the meantime I swung up into the saddle of my horse and prepared to return to the castle with him.

I tried not to dwell on the fact that Haret was there.

The return to Fyalsorn was a nightmare. Ryfik pushed the column until full dark. He wouldn't have halted then if three horses hadn't stumbled in less than five minutes, breaking their legs in the jumble of river rock we were trying to navigate.

"Call a halt, Father," Gosfik called out finally. His father reluctantly agreed.

The encampment was cold, wet, and windy. No fires were allowed lest the Dalgiri spot them. Even if the portal was currently closed—a question Dal would have to address when he caught up with us—and the Neanderthals had no shuttle, their aircars would make short work of us if we were spotted.

The troop was in a foul mood the next morning at reveille. We were in the saddle by first light and thereafter paused only every hour or so to change horses.

We spotted smoke on the horizon halfway through the morning, and then there was no holding the men back. We reached Fyalsorn-Daya just before noon.

Most of the fires in the town had long since burned out, leaving masses of blackened ruins filled with smouldering charcoal. The smell of charred timber hovered over the town strong enough almost to mask the smell of its sewers. *Almost*.

Ryfik didn't even slow down. He clattered over rubble-strewn cobblestone, past dazed townspeople, leaving his troop strung out for nearly a mile behind.

A quick glance around the courtyard of Fyalsorn Castle showed that the fortress had suffered the same fate as the town. The keep had been burned out. A score of corpses lay in a neat row next to the remains of the steam engine, while others were beneath the rubble of the castle's south wall, which had been breached by a massive explosion.

As we pulled our sweating horses to a halt, the quiet man I had dubbed the Commanding General rushed up to Ryfik. His face was contorted in pain and his right arm hung useless at his side. Local medical technology being what it was, I knew I was looking at a walking dead man.

"Lord, thank the gods!"

"Report, Warough. What happened?"

The story came out almost too fast for me to follow. Three aircars had appeared above the castle about the same time we had arrived at the wreck. A voice from the lead car demanded a parley. Warough refused and the Dalgiri had opened fire.

The aircars' initial volley had sliced the roof from a gun tower on the far side of Fyalsorn. An aircar had then landed while another sprayed covering fire throughout the courtyard. The third had attacked the town. After five minutes or so, the grounded car lifted off and all three converged on the tower where Haret and I had been held prisoner.

In the meantime, Warough had organized a defense of the main Keep and wondered at the Dalgiri tactics. I shook my head sadly. If unusual for Fyalsorn, the Dalgiri tactics were crystal clear to me.

Their primary mission had been to find the Taladoran castaways and they had gone about it in the most straight-forward manner possible. The crew of the first aircar interrogated some hapless gunner while the support cars kept the defenders' heads down. When they had the information they came for, all three cars had gone after Haret.

Four Dalgiri blasted through the courtyard wall into the tower, then fought their way up the spiral staircase to Haret's quarters. In the process they left twenty defenders dead—including poor, stooped Argor. Warough wasn't sure, but he thought one Dalgir was carrying another over his shoulders when the raiding team returned to the cars. The two remaining Dalgiri had been seen forcing Haret into an aircar, and the little armada had lifted back into the sky.

Afterward, the aircar carrying Haret disappeared in the direction of the research station while the other two made several more passes at the castle and town to underline their displeasure.

When Warough finished his tale, Lord Ryfik took a long slow look around him, taking in the destruction of ten generations of labor. He turned to me, horror in his eyes. "How many were there?"

I licked dry lips, wondering again if I had misjudged the man. "Three aircars? Perhaps twelve to sixteen, Lord."

"*Sixteen* warriors have wreaked this upon us? What did the people of Fyalsorn do to deserve the plague you have visited upon us, stranger?"

I searched for something to say. Like many before him, Ryfik's first encounter with Paratime civilization had not been to his benefit.

Finally, I sighed deeply and clasped his shoulder. "I know how you feel, Lord. We poor dumb outtimers seemed destined to get stepped on in this universe, don't we?"

Dal and his pack train arrived the next morning. By that time, Ryfik's sense of helplessness had been replaced by burning anger. Dal arrived to find a Council of War in session among the ruins.

I quickly reported everything that had happened. I was on the brink of tears when I broke the news about Haret.

"Calm yourself," he said. "She is conditioned against psych probing. The Dalgiri will not try to question her until they can get her back to the Empire. Now tell me what our friend Ryfik has planned."

The plan was simple. Ryfik had sent riders to the neighboring lords with a levy for warriors. In some cases he was calling in IOUs of twenty years' standing. In three weeks or so, those summoned would rendezvous at Fyal-sorn and march on the Dalgiri station, overwhelming it with sheer strength of numbers if need be.

"It won't work," Dal said, frowning.

"Why not?"

"Because the Dalgiri are isolated from their home timelines at the moment. The portal is closed again. It reopens in two Tendays. We must be in position to attack as soon as the shuttle arrives to take Haret back to Dalgir."

"Attack when a shuttle is here? Are you crazy?"

He looked at me as one does those poor unfortunates who can't be trusted with sharp objects. Finally, he spoke: "If we attack before a shuttle arrives, how are we going to get home?"

I opened my mouth to reply, then closed it again while Dal outlined his plan.

The one time a transtemporal shuttle is vulnerable to attack is when it is grounded. Haret and I had had our aircar shot down back on Salfa Prime by a weapon designed to burn out shuttle lift-and-drive engines. We could never burn out an operating drive, but if we could catch a shuttle on the ground we might be able to interfere with its generators enough to keep it there. And as long as it was grounded, a shuttle could not effectively use the heavy weapons that it carried.

Building a disrupter should be easy with the spare parts Dal had brought back from the wreck. What I couldn't figure out was how he expected such a crude, short-range device to do any good. "Who's going to sneak this thing in through the perimeter alarms and radar-controlled beamers, Dal?"

Dal grinned. "I was thinking of a catapult."

CHAPTER 10

THE rain, which had pelted us sporadically since midnight, finally drizzled to a halt and ghostly tendrils of fog were beginning to edge their way into the valley below. A layer of low clouds reflected back the perimeter lights of the cluster of domes on the valley floor, casting a surrealistic pattern of brightness and inky shadow over the hills where we lay in wait.

I raised my night-vision glasses and quickly scanned the forest before me. Somewhere down there, just at the edge of that circle of light, were a thousand armed and armored men. To each side I could hear the muffled preparations of the cannoneers, and from behind me, the low hiss of steam being vented as the catapult crew waited for dawn.

I stifled a sneeze and glanced at my wrist chronometer. Less than thirty seconds now. Beside me Ryfik watched the general lightening of the leaden overcast as dawn broke on the world above the clouds. Nothing moved among the cluster of silver domes. None of the research-station personnel had been seen since midnight, when we had taken up our positions.

Two Tendays had passed since our return from *Concorde*'s remains. The three weeks had been the busiest, most worrisome, of my life. Not an hour went by that one of us—Dal, Ryfik, Gosfik, or I—wouldn't glance nervously at the sky expecting to see the black shape of a Dalgiri shuttle materialize from the blanket of clouds overhead.

Between bouts of dread, we worked at the gargantuan task of moving in secret nearly a thousand fighting men the fifty miles to the research station. They rode in groups of six or seven, keeping to the deep woods. We sent riders to the neighboring castles—each more than a hundred miles away—to guide their contingents to the rendezvous points. By the seventeenth day, our cavalrymen were strung out all through the mountains. Each company was commanded by an officer with orders to shoot the first man who dared to start a fire.

The operation would have been impossible if the weather hadn't been on our side. It remained typically nasty through the whole period. The Dalgiri manning the station were technicians and garrison troops, and apparently unenthusiastic when it came to mounting patrols in a cold, wet drizzle.

For three days our army, our batteries of cannon, and our catapult stayed hidden in the cold, wet forest while we waited for word that the portal to the Dalgiri timelines was open. Just before dark on the third day, our scouts galloped into camp with the news that a shuttle had grounded at the Dalgiri base.

Our forces sprang to with the skill of men born to military action, taking up position just beyond the station's lighted perimeter, moving like a legion of ghosts in the night. And when we were in position, we each bundled against the cold and damp, made peace with our gods . . . and waited for dawn.

I glanced down at my chronometer for the last time, counting down the seconds to zero hour.

"Three . . . two . . . one—now!"

A loud *whip, crack, hiss* sounded behind me as a dozen dark objects arced overhead to the target. I held my breath as I watched the small, black disruptor cubes land among the lighted domes.

The initial catapult load was a signal to the big field guns that lined the ridge on both sides of my position. The pale gray of the scene was split by a long echo of rolling thunder followed by the whistling scream of chain shot. Huge blue smoke rings floated lazily before each hidden gun, adding to the surrealism of the scene below me. The staccato *pop* of individual small arms rose to a crescendo and then fell off as the musketmen hastily reloaded their weapons.

A thousand screaming men suddenly rose from hiding and charged into the smoke and haze of the valley floor, firing as they went. Very soon it became impossible to see anything of the action except for the flash of musketry and an occasional beamer bolt near the perimeter. Behind us, the catapult let fly again, this time tossing a barrel-size warhead that exploded at the top of its arc. The battle was suddenly pelted with a shower of metal foil made by tearing insulation robbed from *Concorde* into long thin strips. We hoped the chaff would confound the Dalgiri sensors controlling the perimeter weapons.

I climbed to my feet, stretching my legs to get the kinks out, as Dal clambored up the hill from where he had been directing the catapult fire. Like me, he was dressed in full Fyalsornan armor and held an oversized musket in his hands.

"Good shooting," I said. "All the packets came down within the perimeter."

"Let's hope they were close enough to that shuttle to do some good. Shall we join the fight?"

It wasn't exactly the way I had pictured my entry into battle. Dal, Ryfik, and I walked calmly down the far side of the hill and into the carnage below.

I suddenly found myself very busy trying to stay alive. I ran through the smoke and haze toward the sound of firing. Once a soundless bolt of lightning flashed overhead so close that I could feel the heat and smell the ozone. I crouched lower and ran faster.

I quickly neared the grounded shuttle and could make out someone firing a beamer through the open hatchway, pinning down thirty of our riflemen, who in turn were firing into the shuttle interior trying to ricochet a ball into the defender. I hesitantly glanced around the corner of the low wall I had taken cover behind and saw the reason the Dalgiri hadn't closed the hatch.

Three bodies lay half in the hatchway. One was a Dalgir, probably shot while trying to dislodge the two Fyalsornans who had jammed the hatch originally. I glanced around to ask Dal for his advice and discovered he wasn't there. A bit nervous, I turned back to the scene of battle.

A bluish glow caught my eye.

Lying just below the open hatchway, beneath the rising curve of the shuttle hull, was a Dalgiri beamer. I whispered instructions to the man nearest me, and backed hurriedly from the low wall.

My plan was simple. If I could reach the aft end of the shuttle, I would stand a good chance of making it to the beamer without being seen by the defender inside. I wasn't sure what I would do with the beamer once I got it. If nothing else, I should be able to keep that lone marksman's head down.

I zigzagged to the shuttle without incident then crawled beneath the curve of the hull. Progress was glacial. I slowly moved forward a few feet, then rested for a second while I regained my will to go on. The attacking warriors noticed me when I was halfway to the open hatch and they increased their rate of covering fire while I made the last few yards.

Then I was beneath the hatch, still hidden from the Dalgir by the hull contour, and the beamer was in my hand. It was warm to the touch as I checked its charge. The last owner must not have had much of a chance to use it. The charge was maximum.

Steeling myself, I nodded to my friends. They opened up with everything they had, forcing the lone Dalgir defender to duck out of the line of fire long enough for me to hose the inner chamber with the beamer bolts.

Suddenly it was done and the warriors were running toward me through the acrid blue haze that hung over the battlefield. Each one was screaming at the top of his lungs. They didn't even wait for the hatch chamber to cool off, but plunged recklessly into the heat shimmer, their cries of triumph echoing through the shuttle's passageways.

I waited for a few seconds, to get my heart out of my throat, then followed.

After the battle for the shuttle was won, things began to grow quiet. I left six men inside the Dalgiri ship, showing them how to close the hatch once we had cleared the bodies out of the way, warning them not to come out until ordered to do so. Then I gathered my troops—now more than fifty—and went looking for other enemies to conquer.

By this time, there weren't many. As we searched each dome, it became clear that the Dalgiri numbered fewer than a hundred and that we had taken them completely by surprise. Most had died in clothing hastily pulled on and carelessly secured. Many had been cut down as they tried to reach defensive positions throughout the complex. The few who succeeded in making it to their posts had been dug out by small parties of musketmen acting on their own initiative.

When the number of Dalgiri survivors seemed less than a dozen and we called for their surrender, beamer blasts flashed in the defenders' positions. When a few brave Fyalsornans went in to investigate, they found the enemy dead at their own hands.

The war between Dalgir and Talador yields few prisoners.

As soon as we were reasonably sure the Dalgiri resistance had broken, I took a small party and began searching the domes for Haret. My helpers took a perverse delight in their work. There had been relatively little swordplay during the battle because few Fyalsornans had gotten close enough to live Dalgiri to wield their favorite weapon. Their disgruntlement was quickly dispelled when I set them to chopping through interior partitions.

It had been almost forty minutes since I had heard the last musket discharge when Saurzon, the burly eight-foot giant helping me, smashed a door in and an excited female voice called out from the bare cell inside.

"Haret!" I screamed as I lunged past Saurzon and swept her into my arms.

"Oof, careful of my ribs."

"Sorry. Are you all right?"

She gave a little shudder of horror inside the shapeless "hospital gown" the Dalgiri had given her. "I am now. It was a bad night knowing that shuttle had arrived to take me back to Dalgir."

"It's over now," I hugged her once more. "Let's get something suitable for you to wear and find Dal and Ryfik."

Fyalsornan attire was out of the question—hopelessly oversized for Haret's relatively diminutive figure. We found some Dalgiri outerwear in a closet and she slipped into that. Saurzon surrendered his coat to cover the Dalgir uniform, lest she be shot by mistake in the confusion outside.

We located Ryfik and Dal at the shuttle. Dal had just finished an inspection of the interior and stood outside with a puzzled look on his face. Then he saw Haret and went wild with joy. Five hulking Fyalsornans clustered around us and watched the hugging, openmouthed while tears poured down the Taladorans' cheeks.

I let the celebration go on for a minute or so before clearing my throat loudly enough to get Dal's attention. "What's the matter with the shuttle? It's operational, isn't it?"

He released Haret and turned to face me. "From what I've seen, yes. But it's not of any Dalgiri shuttle class that I've ever heard of. Besides the usual lift-and-drive and temporal generators, there are a completely new set of controls and generators installed in the engine room. According to the ship's log, it is one of two shuttles based at this station. Care to guess where the other is?"

"The shuttle that attacked the Academy!" Haret exclaimed. "Then this shuttle is designed to make the jump between universes without going through a transtemporal portal. We've succeeded in our mission."

"I hope so," Dal said, "but there is much that needs to be explained. Why did the crew wait for the local portal to open before returning to base? What do those extra generators do, and what is all the special equipment for?"

"Special equipment?" I asked.

Dal nodded. "They're bringing some of it out now."

Two warriors appeared in the hatchway, each carrying an example of the mysterious "special equipment" in his arms.

"What are they?" Haret asked. "Deep-sea diving suits?"

Dal shrugged. "A more likely use would be protection for working with poison gasses or dangerous biologicals."

I stared at the two Fyalsornans and their prizes, then at Dal and Haret. Suddenly their confusion was too much for me and I collapsed in a fit of laughter, sinking to the wet ground. When I could look up, Haret was leaning over me with concern in her eyes. I broke up once more. After a minute or two I had stopped chuckling long enough to climb to my feet and wipe the tears from my eyes.

"Are you okay, Duncan?" Dal asked.

I nodded, staring at the fluorescent orange and green constructs each warrior held before him. I had recognized the objects instantly. They weren't exactly NASA issue, but the "special equipment" the two Fyalsornan warriors cradled in their arms were obviously a couple of space-suits.

CHAPTER 11

THE Sun was setting behind the mountains to the west, painting a glorious golden backdrop that splashed amber flame across the roofs of the still deserted Time Watch Academy. After months of monotonous gray skies on the Fyalsornan timeline, seeing a real sunset again was like being reborn.

I turned from the wall of glass on the topmost floor of Academy Headquarters and nervously paced a well-worn path in front of the window. The two Taladoran Marines who flanked the only exit watched me impassively. I hardly noticed them anymore. They had become part of the furniture.

My attention was focused instead on a second door, behind which the Emergency Committee of the Ruling Council had been in session for nearly eight hours. Meanwhile, I had been confined to the anteroom with nothing to do but pace or stare out into the Salfa Prime wilderness.

The waiting hadn't been so bad while Haret was locked in my plush prison with me. But Haret had been summoned three hours earlier and had yet to emerge. I hadn't seen Dal Corst at all. Presumably, he had been in the Council meeting from the start.

Suddenly the door opened and a dark man in the uniform of a Commander of the Time Watch entered the anteroom. "We are ready for you now, Watchman."

I sighed. "I guess I'm ready, too."

"Follow me, please."

The Council was using the same conference room in which Dal had originally briefed us on the Fyalsorn mission. Dal and Haret sat poker-faced against one wall, neither looking at me, while I was directed to the end of the long table at which a dozen worthies sat. As I looked at the double row of expectant faces, I was surprised to discover that I recognized some of them. At the head of the table sat Tasloss, Chairman of the Council.

"Please be seated, Watchman," he said, looking even more harried than he had the day I was summoned to his office in Capitol Complex.

"Thank you, sir."

"Your compatriots have briefed us on what took place during your mission, Watchman. We will want a full report from you later. At the moment, however, this Council is more interested in how you came to the conclusion that the special suits found in the shuttle were for use in vacuum."

I shrugged. "They were spacesuits. They couldn't have been anything else. They had globe helmets, backpacks with air tanks on them, pressure seams and gaskets obviously designed to hold pressure in, not out. I recognize a spacesuit when I see one."

A man with auburn hair and yellow skin leaned forward. "Then you were familiar with the possibilities of travel beyond the atmosphere prior to joining the Watch?"

I frowned. "Surely, sir, Dal has explained my . . . uh, origins."

"He has, but we would prefer to hear from your own lips how you solved this mystery, Watchman."

"Yes, sir. Well, as you know, I come from a skewline which has yet to discover crosstime travel. Since Paratime is unavailable to us, we have turned our attentions outward, toward space. We've landed men on the Moon and inhabited rudimentary space stations. So, you might say that I'm familiar with the possibilities.

"Now Dal, Haret, and I talked a great deal about Paratime during the week we waited for the Fyalsornan portal to open, and I learned that portal formation depends in part on the local curvature of space in each universe—I even asked about the possibility of transitioning between congruent points in the same universe. Those discussions must have been percolating around my head the whole time we were guests of Lord Ryfik, because when I saw the two Fyalsornan warriors carrying the spacesuits, everything fell neatly into place."

"Do you have such intuitive flashes often, Watchman?" That from a sharp-faced woman sitting to my right. I recognized her garb as that of an Hereditary Priestess of Muliphoor, whose order was reputed to be one of the finest collections of minds in Paratime.

"No, ma'am. This was my first. I suddenly realized that the Earth isn't the only mass in space that can promote portal formation. And if the Dalgiri need spacesuits, it must be because they are operating beyond the atmosphere. The closest planetary mass to the Earth is the Moon, of course. Once your mind makes that jump, it's a straight shot to the fact that there are temporal portals on the moon, portals which the Dalgiri are using to transit from one timeline to another.

"From what I'd learned about temporal physics, that made more sense than the theory that they had found a method of jumping the barrier between universes—*that* trick would require the power of a good-sized sun. If the Dalgiri had such a shuttle, they wouldn't need to penetrate the barrier; they could force any portal in the Confederation no matter how well defended."

Tasloss shot me a look from the other end of the table. "So you concluded that the Dalgiri had developed teleportation as a means of getting to the Moon?"

"No sir, not at first. I thought they were using their lift-and-drive engines and doing it the same hard way my own people did. It was only after nearly a Tenday of study that we identified the strange engines in that shuttle as teleportation generators, and traced the circuits to the automated guidance computer that controlled them. After that, it was just a matter of experimenting with the controls. We soon found our hearts in our throats and the shuttle hovering over a lunar plain at one-sixth gravity. We couldn't stay long, as the battle had damaged the shuttle's airtightness. Our ears began to pop almost immediately as air leaked out through ruptures in the hatch seals. Dal pushed the teleportation button again, and we found ourselves back on Salfa Prime on the opposite side of the world from the Academy. We flew all night, set down at the shuttle port, and called for assistance.

"And here we are."

"Hah!" The exclamation exploded from a portly gentleman seated on Tasloss's immediate right. He had taken no apparent interest in the conference to this moment, choosing instead to fiddle with the jeweled necklace he wore. There was no mistaking the look of triumph on his face now, however.

"What have I been telling you for nearly two years, esteemed colleagues? This young man's timeline is something special. They are expanding into a field of which we are woefully ignorant. Your caution is laudable, but misplaced. We must act now—*tonight*—before the thousand-times-damned Dalgiri steal another march on us."

"I beg your pardon, Councilor?" I asked with a sinking feeling in the pit of my stomach. "What are you talking about?"

The fat man rose ponderously, his manner that of a politician about to make an important campaign speech. "I propose that we vote this very bora on the admission of the Europo-American timeline into the fellowship of our glorious Confederation. Should the Council see fit to vote with me, the contact fleet will be on its way to your home within a Tenday."

I nodded then stood wearily. I had half expected something like this to happen. I took a deep breath, knowing the rest of my life would be changed by what happened in the next few moments.

"Over my dead body!"

Pandemonium broke out around me. For an instant, I was no longer an active participant in the debate, but rather a disinterested observer inspecting a tableau in a wax museum.

Tasloss was transfixed in the act of banging the table with a stylized mace—a Taladoran gavel—in a vain attempt to restore order. Half the Councilors held their fists out to me—or used less recognizable gestures to show their displeasure—while the others sat back, seemingly to observe their colleagues. Haret sat aghast in her chair, staring at me with horror; while Dal was in midstride, having crossed half the distance between us.

Then Dal was at my side and the spell was broken.

"What the hell are you doing, MacElroy?" he whispered harshly in English.

"Protecting my homeland from avaricious strangers."

He seemed to think about it for a second, and then nodded. "Maybe you've got a point, there." With that, he turned and retook his seat.

After a few minutes, order was restored around the long conference table. When Tasloss spoke, it was with an obvious effort to restrain himself. "Would you care to explain your comments, Watchman? I should think you would be pleased at the prospect of your fellow timeliners obtaining the benefits of Taladoran civilization centuries earlier than planned."

"I'm not sure I can, sir—explain, that is—but I'll try. My main objection is that it is *Taladoran* civilization that you offer us. You offer your way of doing things, not ours. Our civilization would be overwhelmed.

"I was with Lord Ryfik when he discovered Fyalsorn Castle destroyed. His reaction was very enlightening. Oh, he cursed the Dalgiri for the low lifes that they are. But he cursed Talador with equal vehemence. As far as Ryfik is concerned, you and the Near Men are from the same mold. He isn't interested in your petty quarrels. He just wants to be left alone. And you know something? *I know precisely how he feels!*"

Tasloss looked at me down the length of the table. "I think you exaggerate, Watchman."

"Do I? What about my own case? I helped you people to defeat your enemies. What thanks did I get? —I was given the choice between a partial brain burn or a press-ganging into your Paratime operatives. A hell of a way to say thanks if you ask me. Do you want to know why I chose the Time Watch? Because I was told the Dalgiri would be flooding through into my timeline in another couple of decades and I hoped I might stem the tide. I gave up everything to help my people avoid what happened to Ryfik!"

"You made the right decision," someone growled.

"Did I? If I had stumbled into the Dalgiri first, what would have stopped me from joining them? Indeed, what difference would it have made? It seems that Europo-

American's twenty years of grace is going to be cut to a little more than a week no matter what I do.

"Those, ladies and gentlemen, are the facts from my point of view. As has been pointed out to me several times recently, Europo-American has something unique. We are spreading into space, pushing back a frontier which you never realized existed. You would abort that effort, applying all our energy to your war with the Dalgiri, making us carbon copies of yourselves. In short, you would smother us and make us another barely civilized line among hundreds."

I paused for breath, noting the shocked look on their faces. It was as if I'd told a national convention of the D.A.R. that I wished the *Mayflower* had never sailed. I didn't give them time to recover.

"Oh, it has been one hell of an education, I've got to give you that! I've learned that nations can't always do what is right, only what is expedient. So in the name of expedience, let's talk about Talador's reasons for not annexing Europo-American.

"You people have suddenly discovered that Earth is not alone in supplying access to the vastness of Paratime. For some reason, you are surprised to learn that the laws of temporal physics extend throughout the universe. We know there are portals on the Moon. What about the rest of the planets? Don't they also curve space? Think of Mars . . . or Venus . . . or giant Jupiter. How many cross-connections between timelines are there to be found in that vast maelstrom of poison clouds?

"And that's not all! There are a hundred billion stars in our Galaxy. How many of *them* have planets? Can you be sure that something bigger and meaner than *Homo sapiens* isn't lurking out there, even now making ready to pounce?

"The possibilities are limitless. You talk so blithely of the endlessness of Paratime. You have no true concept of infinity until you've spent a cold winter's night staring into the eyepiece of a telescope and recognized what you were looking at. Alternate universes may be infinite in number, but space . . . that is the greater infinity!"

Dal smiled. Excitement was visible in his expression. He was getting the message. Tasloss cleared his throat, suddenly uncomfortable. Maybe I was getting to him too.

"It would seem to me, Watchman, that you have just made the case for the immediate annexation of your timeline. If the danger is as great as you say, we must control your people's expertise at any cost."

I shook my head. "You aren't thinking it through. Our space program is in its infancy—we have barely made it to the Moon. What happens when you undermine our efforts by revealing that there is no need to go to the planets? You have been seduced by your thousands of lovely, exploitable Earths. What makes you think we are made of stronger stuff than you? Why would anyone risk his skin in a vacuum-packed sardine can when he can have a temporal shuttle to ferry him between a limitless series of Earthly paradises?

"Abort spaceflight now, and it seems to me you'll be stuck with an infant technology that will never advance. You will be able to guard the Moon adequately on all your timelines, but the Sun, the stars, and the planets will remain forever beyond your capabilities. Wouldn't it be better to slow the annexation of Europo-American? You should at least delay until we've developed spaceflight to the point where you can guard the Solar System on your timelines. After all, nothing will prevent you from siphoning off our technology in secret. Consider it a controlled experiment in an alternate way of looking at the universe, if you will."

The Councilor who had originally proposed annexing Europo-American drummed his fingers on the table and glared at me. "If it is inherently impossible for a Paratime civilization to develop space travel, Watchman, how do you explain the Dalgiri having done so?"

"Simple!" a familiar voice boomed out. "They didn't!" I was startled to discover that the voice was mine.

"Explain that comment."

I licked dry lips, feeling many of the same emotions I had felt during the interview with Lord Ryfik. My mouth had gotten me into a tight spot, and now it was up to my mouth to get me out. I thought furiously as I stalled for time. Suddenly, I had the answer.

"The Dalgiri didn't discover space travel. They tripped over it in their travels crosstime, the same as you did. I should have realized it before now. The teleportation controls in their shuttle are too simple. You push a button and find yourself on the Moon. You push it again and you're in another timeline back on Earth. Even the Russians give their crews more control than that. There should have been some kind of manual backup in case the automatics failed. There weren't any because the Dalgiri don't truly understand the mechanics of teleportation. If they don't understand it, they certainly didn't invent it. Therefore, they must have stolen it somewhere."

I paused for breath and found myself out of arguments. Tasloss stared ponderously up and down the table before facing me. "Thank you for your opinions, Watchman. Please wait in the next room while we make our decision."

I rose unsteadily to my feet and started for the door. I couldn't shake the feeling that I had blown it with my big mouth. One last glance convinced me. From the looks on their faces, it was obvious that I had lost.

A rough hand brought me awake with a start. I looked up. Dal was leaning over me. I frowned. The last thing I remembered was sitting down because my feet hurt. The Council was still in session two hours after they had kicked me out, the argument sometimes overpowering the conference room's soundproofing.

"Don't tell me I went to sleep," I groaned. "My whole world is at stake and I can't even keep my eyes open."

"That was one helluva performance you put on in there. You deserve the rest," Dal said in English.

"Well? Don't keep me in suspense. Do I go back to hitting the books at dear old Time Watch U. or do I pack my bags for Leavenworth?"

"Neither."

"Huh?"

I scanned Dal's expression for a clue to my future. He refused to give me one. Then, after an agonizing ten seconds, he let his lips curl up in a slow smile.

"You did it! The annexation has been called off."

I let out a yell that rattled the wall of glass next to me. I would have danced a jig if I hadn't been so tired.

"It wasn't an easy decision, mind you," he continued. "They were ready to kill each other after you left. Luckily, everyone cooled down and reason more or less prevailed.

"The Committee will recommend that the full Council accept your suggestion and let Europo-American develop without interference. Not that we are abandoning the timeline, you understand. We're doubling our force of agents there. The plan is to saturate your high-technology industries with crosstime spies. They will report back on every phase of your space program, allowing us to copy any developments that look promising. Spacesuit design is first on the list, by the way."

"Sounds promising, Dal."

"You don't mind a little surreptitious recruiting, do you?"

"No, I guess not."

"Good, because they also decided Europo-American is a good source for new Watchmen. You've shown us that we have become a bit inbred and are in desperate need of new blood and ideas. Of course, we are going to bend all of our efforts toward keeping the Dalgiri off the line, too. Wouldn't be much of a controlled experiment if we allowed them to kick hell out of you people in a couple of decades, would it?"

"Most decidedly not."

Dal chuckled. "You should have seen old Tasloss toward the end. He looked like he had the weight of all Paratime on his shoulders. He's spent his life keeping the barbarians at bay and you just exposed a new panorama of dangers he never realized existed. Now he has to start over, rebuilding his defense perimeter. It will be the work of millennia to calm the fears you raised in there today, Duncan. I hope you're proud of yourself."

I grinned. "You know something, Dal? I really am. I joined the Watch for a lot of reasons, some of which I can't even explain to myself. But mostly I joined to try and protect Europo-American. If that means getting kicked out of the Time Watch, so be it."

"Who's being kicked out?"

"Well, I assumed if I'm not returning to my studies here at the Academy, that I was out on my ear."

"What gave you that idea? We need you. The Council is launching a crash program to fortify the Moon on each of our timelines. They're throwing all of the resources of the Confederation into the project—'getting nine women pregnant to produce a baby in one month' is the expression I believe I heard once on Europo-American. We're going to need the services of every expert on heavy construction in a vacuum that we can find. And if I'm not mistaken, the number of people in the Confederation who meet the qualifications can be counted on the thumbs of one hand—and they're all named Duncan MacElroy!"

"Heavy construction? Vacuum? What do I know about either?"

"More than any of us—I hope. But don't worry. You won't be at it long. When the Council decrees a crash program, things move amazingly fast. Within six months the engineers should know enough about working in vacuum to let you go. As soon as they do, you're coming with me. I'm arranging an expedition to find the timeline that supplied Dalgir with the teleportation trick. Who knows, if they are like Dalgir's usual client worlds, they may even join us."

"An expedition? Into Dalgiri time?"

Dal nodded. "You *do* want to go, don't you?"

"Of course, I want to go! I promised Ryfik that I would do everything I could to protect him. This sounds like just the thing to keep the Dalgiri too busy to bother him again."

"I can go you one better on that. We're to fortify the Fyalsornan universe with everything available. Can't have Dalgiri shuttles popping up on Salfa Prime all the time, now can we? And thanks to your impassioned plea before the Committee, Haret has been assigned as liaison officer to Ryfik and his people. She will have the job of guarding against the excesses of cultural imperialism you decried so effectively."

"Haret's been reassigned?"

"Didn't I just say that?"

"When is she leaving?"

"Thirty days—why?"

I grinned. "I thought I would invite her swimming in our favorite mountain pool tomorrow. We were interrupted at an inconvenient moment last time. I thought we might take up where we left off."

CHAPTER 12

DAL was right about one thing. When the Ruling Council decreed that something would be done in the shortest possible time, *it was!* But even the Council couldn't work miracles.

After six months, the Lunar-fortification project was barely begun. It takes time to put a new and radically different technology into place, even when the design and fabrication of equipment is mostly the work of computers.

The weak link, as usual, was people.

The scientists, engineers, technicians, and workers had to be taught to think in new ways. It was as if the President had announced in 1962 that the U.S. planned to land a man on the Moon by the end of 1963. The delay was simply a case of insufficient lead time. People have to have the time to think a new idea through.

And then there were delays in the shuttle-modification program. Every shipbuilding facility in the Confederation dropped whatever it had been doing and began to install teleportation generators in the ships of the Taladoran Navy (as well as the life-support modifications essential for operations in space). Trouble was, there weren't enough shipyards to go around. And then there were the usual delays inherent in any program where development and production are proceeding concurrently. Every month or so modifications had to be made to the modifications in order to fix new problems uncovered during flight tests of the captured shuttle.

Finally, though, enough spaceworthy shuttles were ready and a hasty survey was made of all the Moons of the Confederation. We learned that fully nine out of ten universes had active lunar portals—some as many as three. The survey's findings were greeted as if they were the punch line to a classic good news/bad news joke.

The good news was that the core universes of the Confederation's interdependent timeline cluster had a higher interconnectivity coefficient than anyone had imagined. That meant easier, less circuitous routes from point-of-origin to destination for Taladoran shippers, thus lower costs and a higher standard of living for everyone.

But *every* lunar portal had to be defended, thus magnifying the Watch's problem until it was nearly insurmountable. The Corps of Engineers found itself in the position of having to construct nearly fifty vacuum-proof, heavily armed fortresses all across Paratime in the shortest possible time.

It would have been stretched to the limit by half that number.

Two years after Dal had promised to spring me from durance vile, I found myself on my seventh timeline in less than six months. At the moment in question, I stood broiling under a sun undimmed by atmosphere, my poor tired flesh encased in a smelly vacsuit with an underpowered cooling unit, as I watched six Taladoran technicians struggle to complete the power hookups for the fixed-beamer battery that was our sole means of defense. The place was Anaxagoras Crater in the northern lunar highlands on my home timeline of Europo-American. The fixed beamers—and the temporal portal they guarded—were a hundred kilometers away, on the other side of the lunar pole from us.

The Earth—*my Earth*—was a blue-white orb that hovered perpetually just above the southern rim of the crater. Three days before, the sight of that beautiful ball framed against the black velvet of open space had made my long exile almost worth it. No more. I was too uncomfortable at the moment to work up much enthusiasm for world saving. My mind was on more immediate concerns . . . like being hot, sweaty, smelly, minus on my sleep, and generally perturbed about the way my life had been going.

"Duncan MacElroy, report to the base commander's office immediately!" The command erupted from my earphones and bounced around the hollow confines of my helmet. Normally I would have welcomed the opportunity to be free of my vacsuit, but not this time. A few hours of misery was heaven compared to a summons from Garsich Mersaich, the Watchman in charge of making sure that Anaxagoras Base got built soonest.

When you were called before Garsich, you were sure of one thing. You weren't about to be kissed on both cheeks.

"Watchman MacElroy, reporting as ordered."

The grizzled old warrior was hunched over his desk-cum-computer-terminal, and grunted his acknowledgment of my presence.

"What do you know about this satellite your people are lofting next Tenday, MacElroy?"

I hesitated as I changed mental gears. Then I remembered. When the Taladorans had first arrived on the Moon, they found two lunar mappers in orbit—one American, one Russian. Both had been put out of action to keep them from transmitting pictures of our little project back to the men on the ground. The Russians had won the race to prepare a replacement and were even now readying a launch vehicle.

"They're not *my people*. They're Russians," I said, truculently.

"Fellow timeliners, then."

"Well . . ." That was as far as I got as alarms began to clamor all over the place. Garsich vaulted his desk and was gone. I turned to follow and finally caught up with him in the main fortress control room. He was spewing orders at least fifty percent of which were profane.

I also found Jana Dougwaix there. It had been four years since we'd said good-bye forever at Jafta shuttle port, four years that Jana had spent studying the aborigines of Europo-American. As soon as construction began on Anaxagoras Base, however, she had been drafted as the house expert on the local yokels and shipped to the Moon.

"What's going on, Jana?"

"Intruder just came through the portal going like a bat out of hell. They're trying to track it now with inputs from the overhead satellites."

"Identified?"

She nodded, slipping into her Europo-American mannerisms with an ease that betrayed long practice. "Dalgiri, what else?"

With a shock I remembered the work party I had just left. We were defenseless without power to our beamers.

A dozen wall screens were alight with inputs from sensors monitoring the time gate. As I watched all the screens flashed warning messages simultaneously and the alarms sounded again. A second shuttle materialized in empty space.

"Dalgir, same course as Target One!" the detector operator called out.

The new ship gathered speed and disappeared over the horizon. Less than a second later, a map of Lunar Farside flashed on the screens. The second shuttle's course was superimposed on the multicolored map as a glowing red line.

"Any sign of additional shuttles?" Garsich roared as he watched the movement of the second target.

"None," the technician on duty called back.

"Something's wrong here," he said, almost to himself. "That survey was pretty damned quick. Any chance they missed a portal?"

Schruelsin bis Harl-son, Garsich's deputy and the closest thing we had to a temporal physicist, glanced up from his monitoring station. "Not a chance, Gar. We've got a detector satellite in a ball-of-string orbit not much higher than these peaks around us. There is only one area of low temporal potential on this orb, and we're sitting on it."

"Energy discharge, Commander." This from one of the detector technicians following the intruders. "Beamer fire by the spectrum."

"What, by the Square Gods of Lashua, is going on here?"

"Target One reacquired . . . More beamer fire . . . They're fighting each other!" The reports quickly arrived at the Filter Console from the outer circle of detector stations. We could see nothing on our screens but the craggy highlands of Farside and frequent flashes of lightning that overdrove the screen's light-amplification circuits.

"Target Two hit, but returning fire; sensors detect atmospheric gas around its image. . . . Target One taking fire not as bad. *Direct hit!* Target Two has exploded."

The tech's running commentary was unnecessary as we stood riveted to the deck and gaped at the strange sight on our screens. The two Dalgiri shuttles had just fought a slugging match near Mare Moscoviense, and the last through the portal had come up the loser. As we watched, a searing point of light blossomed on the surface of the Moon an instant before the screen went blank.

"Our sensors were burned out by that last one," the tech reported.

"What about the remaining shuttle?" Garsich demanded.

"Damaged. The field scanners report loss of lift-and-drive just before our instruments overloaded. It could be down."

I turned to Jana, who had watched the drama unfold with the same wonder that I had. "Now what-in-hell was that all about?"

"Damned if I know," she said. "I'll bet that old Garsich doesn't wait long to find out, though."

"No bet."

No bet, indeed.

Within fifteen minutes we were down in the hangar bays slipping into our suits. I say we, because Jana and I had been assigned to operate a survey scooter in a sweep of Farside. The scooter was little more than a bench seat big enough for two and a lift-and-drive generator. It was bigger than a single man floater, but not much.

We were vectored with three other search teams to the site of the explosion, but a single look was all it took to conclude that no one had survived that inferno. After satisfying ourselves that the molten slag heap had truly been a Dalgiri shuttle, we split up and began our sweep of the surrounding area.

The four teams separated until each scooter was approximately fifty kilometers from its neighbors, then pivoted our rough line with the center of Mare Moscoviense as our anchor, before beginning a slow traverse down from Tereshkova Crater toward the great splash mark that is Mendeleev. We carried portable detectors that would react to the presence of a Paratime shuttle, even a disabled one—unless, of course, it happened to be in the same condition as the wreck we had just left.

We cruised slowly southward, the surface below us a sea of impact craters. We searched in silence, the only sound that of our breathing, until:

"Hey! I'm getting something on the detector," Jana said. "Veer left, over toward that largish crater on the horizon."

I steered the scooter toward the rocky prominence she referred to, reporting our contact to the others of our search party. We hugged the terrain—lunain?—while Jana interpreted the weak readout on the detector.

"There it is!" I yelled as we topped a crater wall. Lying before us inside a small crater was the Dalgiri shuttle. It had hit hard. The hull had cracked, and interior light was streaming through the break. If it hadn't been for that, the craft would have been invisible in the semishadow where it lay.

Jana and I landed behind the rocky protuberance that served as a central peak of the nameless crater. We waited until the other three parties had converged on us, then approached the wreck. I signaled Jana to stay under cover and then levered myself through the break, feeling very vulnerable as I did so. Fortunately, the shuttle was deserted.

I had been exploring the interior for ten minutes when Jana called on the comlink and reported footprints in the dust outside. I hurriedly left the shuttle and joined her near where a long rille broached the crater wall and snaked off into deep shadow.

Sure enough, two sets of bootprints headed up the narrow valley. We reported the trail to the others, switched on our flashlamps, and followed. Before we had gone many yards, it was clear that one of the survivors was injured. One set of prints trailed its right leg while the other grew alternately deeper and shallower. I'm no Indian scout, but I quickly figured the latter prints were made by someone supporting the injured party every few paces.

As we entered the rille, we moved from the blinding brightness of direct sunlight into the shadow of the narrow cut. Jana and I paused to let our faceplate polarizers adjust to the new level of ambient light. While we waited for our pupils to adapt to the sudden dark, we fingered our beamers and peered into the blackness ahead.

"What do you think?" I asked.

"I think we need more people."

"Want to call two of the scooters down from the rim?"

She turned to face me and shook her head silently. Translation: *What's the sense in all of us getting killed?* We then walked farther into the lion's den, each step taking us closer to our wounded, armed, and probably dangerous quarry.

Suddenly Jana halted and swung her flashlamp to the right. I followed with my spot. Ahead of us, the bootprints entered an angular split in the rock that was almost a cave. "I guess we check it out, Duncan." Jana's voice was strained.

We crunched our way to the cave, taking care to avoid the line of fire of anyone inside. We turned off our comm units and put our helmets together for a hurried conference. After a brief argument, Jana agreed to position herself to the side of the slit.

Three seconds later, she switched her flash to high beam and wide dispersal and pointed it into the cave while shielding most of her body behind the wall of rock. At the same instant I dove through the entrance, landing on my belly with my beamer extended in what I hoped was authentic wild-west style.

"Don't shoot!" I screamed.

Directly ahead of me and not ten feet away were two figures in Dalgiri spacesuits. But the people in them weren't Dalgiri. At least, the one whose face was turned outward toward the light was no Neanderthal. I had seen dozens of Dalgiri and not one had sported a pert button nose, soft red lips, or a beautiful heart-shaped face framed by cascades of jet-black hair.

CHAPTER 13

I lay in the dust of the cave, my heart pounding in my ears, for perhaps ten seconds. The woman stared at me through the darkening filter of her helmet as her lower lip quivered in fright. She cradled the other figure protectively in her arms. I tore my gaze from her face and scanned for weapons. She seemed unarmed.

Jana covered me while I got to my feet, holstering my beamer as I did so. The woman's eyes followed my movement. Her mouth opened and her lips moved in silent speech. I chinned my comm to the general channels.

"—don't hurt us. Please don't hurt us." The voice was a pleasant contralto made hard by panic.

The language was Dalgiri.

"Don't worry, you are safe with us," I responded in the same language. I walked forward, keeping my hands in sight, to get a better look at the other figure. The man was of the same race as the girl and unconscious. A trickle of blood ran from the corner of his mouth, disappearing into a sparse, black beard.

The woman said something I didn't quite understand. The language was still that of the Near Men, but the words were burdened by an accent I didn't recognize.

I reached out to pat her on the shoulder through the heavy material of her suit, hoping that it was as much a gesture of reassurance on her timeline as it was on mine.

"We won't hurt you," I said again in Dalgiri, forming the words slowly and carefully so there would be no misunderstanding.

She smiled, revealing a set of perfectly formed pearl-white teeth that contrasted sharply with her skin and hair.

"Thank you."

"What is your name?"

"Felira Transtas, Clan Rossa of the People of Syllsin."

I told her my name and gestured to the man: "Who is this?"

"My brother, Graf Transtas. He was injured during our fight with the *Vecka*. Please help him!"

I had no idea what *Vecka* meant, but the inflection she gave it told me it wasn't something you usually heard at a testimonial dinner. I turned to Jana. "I guess we'd better call a shuttle."

She did so before holstering her beamer and walking completely inside. Between us we got the injured man to his feet and I hoisted him over my shoulder in a fireman's carry—not easy to do in a vacsuit, even if the victim weighs only fifty pounds or so. I hoped that I hadn't injured him further with such treatment, but we had to get the man to the crater floor where a shuttle could put down.

Three scooters descended from the guard positions they had taken on the crater rim. Among the other searchers was the base medical officer, Zela Bar from the Varnoth timeline. He bent over the injured man, inspecting his face through the faceplate.

"Shock," he said gruffly as he straightened up. "Probably bleeding internally. That shuttle had better get here fast if we're going to save him."

An hour later a rescue shuttle homed to a landing beside the ruined Dalgiri vessel. It was one of the giant cargo globes that had delivered the raw materials for Anaxagoras Base. While Zela Bar supervised the loading of the wounded man, I explained to the woman that she would be accompanying the doctor and her brother.

"Are you not coming too, Duncan?"

"I have to help the others. Go on, you'll be all right." In seconds she was up the ramp, the cargo carrier's clamshell doors closed behind her, and the ship was heading north.

"Beautiful, isn't she?" a voice said in my earphones. I turned. Jana stood a dozen feet from me, a cryptic expression on her face.

"Who?" I asked.

Jana chuckled. "Who, indeed? Our little castaway, of course."

"Yes," I agreed, nodding. "She is that."

Flight time back to Anaxagoras Base was the same two hours as the trip out. By the time we sighted the big crater on the horizon I was more than ready to doff the smelly balloon I wore, and indulge in an orgy of scratching. There was one place right in the small of my back. . . .

Our four scooters broke formation and lined up single file for landing as a huge section of cliff face swung open, and soft blue light spilled out onto the black-gray-brown lunar surface.

Jana and I were number three to land. We barely waited for the scooter to slide to a halt before we were out of our saddles and racing for the airlock in long, loping strides. Once inside, we took turns undogging each other's pressure seals, making it a contest to see who could get free first. People who wax lyrical about the wonders of space travel have never spent a full day cooped up with themselves in a vacsuit.

"Argghh," I said as Jana helped me lift the torso piece of my suit over my head, and I nearly dislocated a shoulder blade trying to reach the small of my back.

"Here, let me help you," she said, slipping her soft hands under mine. "About there?"

"A little higher . . . now to the right . . . down . . . that's it!"

Few joys in this world are quite so basic as scratching a persistent itch. After I could think clearly again, I returned the favor, my hands roaming playfully over Jana's body. We stood for half a minute, blissfully unaware of our surroundings, our arms entwined and our hands busy.

"Remind you of anything?" I asked softly as I nuzzled her ear. I could feel her lips curve into a smile against my throat.

"That first night in your uncle's cabin," she purred.

"Do you ever wish we could go back there?"

"Sometimes. If only things had been different . . ."

We were interrupted before I could find out what she meant as the annunciator over our heads blared out:

"Watchman MacElroy, report to the Base Commander's office, immediately!"

"Damn. What now?" Since there was no obvious answer to that question, I quickly kissed Jana good-bye then hurried through the great empty bays that would someday hold dormitories and living quarters, but which for now were merely huge echoing caves. In five minutes I was once again in the small office where I had been—just this morning? It seemed more like last year.

"Watchman MacElroy reporting as requested, sir!"

"Good of you to come so quickly, MacElroy," Garsich said, looking up from a message flimsy on his desk. "I just received a communication about you from Headquarters. It says, and I quote: 'The subject Watchman is to be relieved of his duties with your command and is hereby ordered to report for staff duty under Watch Commander Dal Corst to participate in planning a major effort against the Dalgiri.' Know anything about this?"

I nodded. "Dal's finally received the go-ahead for an expedition into the Empire to trace the source of the teleportation generator!"

Garsich smiled, one of the few times I'd ever seen him do so. "Well, good luck. I only wish I were going with you instead of sitting in this Threla-cursed hole bossing a bunch of independent-minded techs. Your transportation priority is routine, I'm afraid, so you will have to wait for the regular supply transport in ten days."

"What about the special shuttle that will be taking the two outtimers to Talador?"

"Gone. Zela Bar felt the injured man needed first-rate medical facilities as soon as he could get them."

I shrugged. "I guess it's the milk run then. By your leave, sir." I turned to go.

"One more thing, MacElroy," Garsich said. "Since you will be around until the next transport anyway, you might as well do something useful."

"Such as?"

"The pesky sky spy your people are lofting is still on schedule and two Paratemporal craft are wrecked on the surface of this worthless rock. It would never do to have them scanned, now would it? I am assigning you to the work party that will clean up that mess. Report to Assistant Pilot Belraem in Airlock A3."

I turned once more to go, then stopped, turning back to face Garsich. "Does this mean I will be working outside in a vacsuit?"

The old warrior looked up from the desk's work screen, his face once again a study in disciplined dourness. "You will be working outside. Whether you wear a suit is up to you. Dismissed."

Cleaning up the mess from the battle of Moscoviense took most of the ten days I had left. Felira's shuttle was relatively easy as it was almost in one piece. The Veckan shuttle, having been spread over several hundred acres of moonscape, as well as having melted a fair-size hole in the lunar rock, was considerably more difficult. Not only did we have to pick up all the pieces and smooth out each tiny crater left behind, we had to erase all footprints and other marks of our presence.

Of course, it was impossible to eliminate *completely* the traces of the accident. If anyone on the ground ever suspected that there were people on the Moon, a determined comparison of the Lunar Orbiter photos of the mid-1960s with those taken more recently would quickly turn up clues to our presence. But we relied on no one's suspecting in the first place. We picked up pieces of shuttle, swept the surface with compressed air, and generally "policed" the area of the more glaring inconsistencies.

We were one tired crew of space janitors that poured from the big cargo shuttle the watch period before I was due to ship for Talador. Jana and I spent the evening together, although I must report that I ungallantly fell asleep in the middle of dinner. She accompanied me to the ship the next morning.

"Take care of yourself, Duncan."

"You take care, too. That's a pretty rough place you've been assigned to up there," I said, hooking my thumb to point in the general direction of the unseen Earth.

"I wish we weren't always saying good-bye to one another."

"Me too," I said. "You started to say something that

day we got back from finding Felira Transtas, remember?"

"What do you mean?"

"You said, 'If only things had been different.' If only things had been different how?"

She sighed. "It was nothing. I was just wondering what we would have done if we'd met under different circumstances. If I hadn't been an agent of the Time Watch, and if you weren't an outtimer destined for greatness. If we had just been two people out for a walk that night . . . would you have looked twice at me?"

I took her in my arms and chuckled. "Not the way you had yourself made up. You were the second ugliest woman I ever met!"

She reddened, and then smiled in spite of herself. "They told me to be unobtrusive."

"That you were."

The tone announcing imminent departure of the supply boat chose that moment to sound.

"Don't do anything foolish, little brother," Jana said as she reached up to kiss me. Afterward, she turned and fled the hangar bay, but not before I had seen the glint of tears in her eyes.

I turned to board the shuttle feeling light-headed. Her kiss had been anything *but* sisterly.

CHAPTER 14

DAL Corst was waiting inside the passenger terminal at Jafta Port after I disembarked from the supply shuttle.

"Welcome back," he said, clapping me on the back. "Enjoy your vacation at home?"

"Ever spent three days in a vacsuit?" I asked.

Dal chuckled. "I thought you wanted to be a spaceman."

I made the expected rude noise in answer to his comment. "Hey, what's this *Watch Commander* Corst business?"

"I've been promoted."

"Congratulations."

"Nothing any other strong-hearted, weak-minded Taladoran boy couldn't have done. Where's your baggage?"

"Damned if I know. They said it had to go through quarantine and that I could pick it up in the terminal."

It took nearly half an hour to get clear of the organized chaos of the port. Eventually Dal led me to an official Confederation aircar parked in a VIP spot. As we approached I could make out that someone was already seated in it.

"Duncan MacElroy, I'd like you to meet my second-in-command, Hral Ssaroth," Dal said.

Dal's deputy, who had been sitting with his back to us as we approached, turned, and I grabbed for the beamer I wasn't wearing. Hral Ssaroth wore the gray uniform of the Taladoran Time Watch, but his features were those of a Dalgir!

Ssaroth noticed my jumpiness and smiled, transforming

his craggy features into a miniature lunar landscape. Dal guffawed behind me.

"Perhaps I should have warned you. Hral is one of our former spies, recently returned from a fifteen-year tour of duty in the Empire. He comes highly recommended. I'm told that it was only through good luck and his own superior ability that he got away with his hide. He's from the Aazmoran timeline."

I grinned and pressed my fists against Ssaroth's. I felt a little stupid at my reaction. Even though Talador's chief opponents are of that branch of humanity known as Neanderthal, that did not disqualify others of their kind from Confederation membership. There were currently three Neanderthal universes in the Confederation. Aazmoran was the most advanced. I had attended the Academy with a number of Aazmorians, and they had been cultured and pleasant people all.

"I apologize, Hral Ssaroth. Dal may have told you that I am an outtimer by birth. I'm afraid I still have a number of quaint customs to unlearn—picking my nose, jumping to conclusions, things like that."

Ssaroth laughed. "I understand, Watchman. It is something that my people have to live with for having the Dalgiri as distant relatives. No offense taken."

Ssaroth took the aircar controls while Dal and I climbed into the closed compartment behind him. We were soon high above the sprawl of Jafta megalopolis. A quizzical look rode Dal's face as he regarded me with violet eyes.

"Duncan, old friend, sometimes you give me pause, you know that?"

"Huh?"

"I have spent every waking hour for the last two years preparing for our expedition into Dalgiri time. It has been hard, tough work, but I have finally begun to pull things together. So what happens? You are exiled to the boondocks, decide to go for a stroll one day, and solve the problem while barely lifting a finger."

"I don't understand."

"You remember a certain young woman of unknown origin you met on the Moon ten days ago? She just happens to be a member of the race that invented the teleportation generator."

"You mean Felira?"

"Yes, I mean Felira. How do you always end up in the right place at the right time?"

I shrugged. "Just lucky, I guess. How's her brother?"

"I'm afraid he didn't make it. The medical report says massive internal injuries."

"Too bad. It must have hit her hard."

"It hit me worse. Those damned medics had her sedated for nearly half a Tenday. I didn't even learn of her existence until three days ago. If they'd let me in on their little secret sooner, I would have had you fetched back special and you wouldn't have had to wait for the supply shuttle."

"So what's the scoop, Dal?"

"Patience . . . All will be explained. I've set up a briefing for you, as I am a little busy right now. Your Felira has burned holes in my plans, and I'm right in the middle of reformulating them."

"She's not *my* Felira," I said, a bit surprised at my own testiness.

Dal got that cryptic look on his face that means he knows something I don't and is enjoying himself too much to let me in on the secret.

"That's what you think," he said, chuckling.

The conference room was empty save for Dal Corst, myself, and a short, dumpy woman with a splotchy red face and a complex pattern of furrows cut in her hair. She had been introduced to me as Soufilcar Jouniel, the staff correlationist who was interrogating Felira Transtas.

"Fil will brief you, Duncan. I've got to run," Dal said. "Too many damned details to wrap up around this place."

With that he was gone. I turned to the woman. "Ready when you are, Academician."

Jouniel pressed a contact on the lectern before her and the lights dimmed. A holoscreen lit up to show a life-size still of Felira's face. She was either drugged or sleeping peacefully.

"Watch Commander Corst thought it best that you view the pertinent parts of our interview with the subject, Watchman. Because of the trauma associated with the loss of her sibling, she has been under narcoquiz most of the time. The excerpt you will see was culled from over forty bora of interviews." Then she punched another stud on the lectern and the face in the cube came to life. Off camera, Jouniel's voice asked Felira her name.

"Felira Rossif Bax Adelphia Transtas, second daughter of Grafftar Bax Transtas, Hereditary Law Speaker of Transtas Sept, Clan Rossa." Her eyes remained closed, but her voice was strong and clear.

Jouniel punched a control and the scene froze again. "Note the ritualistic recitation of her genealogy and, particularly, the stress on family, Watchman. This is a modified clan society with strong family relationships." She set the cube record in motion once again.

A new scene began. Felira lay on the same padded table, with Jouniel somewhere out of camera range. Now the camera angle had widened to show Felira's bare shoulders down to the upward swell of her breasts. The shot wasn't particularly revealing, no more so than hundreds of perfume and hair-spray commercials I'd seen back home. In spite of that, my heart beat faster.

Jouniel asked about Felira's people and the Vecka. Felira stirred in her sleep. Her voice, when it finally came, had a curious quality and it quickly became evident that what we were hearing was an epic saga of her people's history.

Once (so the saga began) the Syllsintaag had been a proud and mighty race, the masters of their world. They had conquered their planet and had begun to gaze up at the stars with a sense of longing.

Then the Vecka had come from nowhere in huge ships to raid and plunder. That had been three hundred years ago. Their takings included machinery, fissiles, and people. And when the ships were bloated with booty, they rose into the blue sky then vanished.

The black ships came every seventh year for the next century. Each time they were more numerous and powerful. Each time more cities were plundered and ever larger numbers of Syllsintaag were taken captive. Between raids those left behind could do nothing but repair the damage and prepare their defenses.

Then, for a period of seventy-five years, the raids stopped and civilization began to rebuild. A Golden Age spread across the world of Syllsin. People began to forget the nightmare they had been through. They grew fat and happy—until, one day, the biggest horde of all appeared in their skies. This time it was no raid.

Ten years of fierce fighting followed during which half the Syllsintaag perished. They fought valiantly, but to no avail. In the end, the Vecka ruled Syllsin with an iron hand.

Jouniel stopped the projector and turned to me. "Of course, you understand that what we are hearing is not an objective account. It is an heroic saga painted in stark white and black, with no effort at moderation. But the backbone of the story, that of the Veck-Syllsin struggle, must be relatively accurate. Does the pattern of the raids remind you of anything, Watchman?"

I nodded. "I'd say a skewline couplet with intermittent portals."

Jouniel smiled. "Dal was right. You are a bright one."

Like Europo-American, Felira's home universe wandered a skewed path through Paratime, touching the vast interdependent timeline clusters infrequently. Unlike Europo-American, however, Syllsin did not wander alone. Apparently, it was one of a couplet. Such relationships are fairly common across Paratime, with the temporal portals between two such lines stable, long-lived affairs. Syllsin had been an exception to the rule. For centuries the time gate from Veck had been an erratic one, opening for only a few days or weeks each decade. Then, as such gates will do, it had closed for four generations, to reopen "permanently" as the swirling pattern of entropic energy stabilized for an eye blink of geologic time.

While the portal was intermittent, the Vecka had to content themselves with brief raids for raw materials and slaves. As soon as the gateway became reliable, however, they had moved in to stay, carving out an Empire in which the Syllsintaag occupied the lower rungs of the ladder.

The hologram began to move again.

"What of the teleportation generator?"

Felira stirred at Jouniel's question, obviously disturbed. "Graf . . . where is Graf?"

"Graf has gone away," Jouniel's voice said gently. "What of the teleportation generator?"

The teleportation generator, it turned out, was the result of a crash program to discover the secret of the black Veckan ships during that last decade of resistance. More than one raider had been bested in battle, damaged, and captured. Yet the great engines remained inert masses of lifeless metal no matter what the Syllsintaag scientists did to them.

"Not surprising," Jouniel said. "Without a portal to use, a temporal generator is so much junk."

But the scientists refused to believe their hard-won prizes did absolutely nothing. So they experimented until a luckless technologist succeeded in making a copy of a Veckan engine disappear. Rather than being transported from Syllsin to an alternate Earth, however, the generator teleported its hapless passenger to the Syllsin moon. Explosive decompression killed him, but not before the automatic return had been activated. The evidence of his body was clue enough to what had happened.

The cube went blank. I turned to Jouniel. "So who are these Vecka and how did the Dalgiri get hooked up with them?"

Jouniel looked surprised, then sheepish. "Didn't I explain that? I guess not. Sorry."

"Well?"

"Isn't it self-evident from the young woman's speech? The Vecka are a small band of refugee Dalgiri."

I mulled that thought over in my head. Something about it didn't feel right, but I couldn't put a name to my feeling.

"Why refugees?" I asked.

"They were after slaves. Why? Machinery is more efficient. Yet their raids were primarily to obtain power-generation equipment and worker-breeding stock. That would only make sense if they were a small group cut off from the mother culture. Since our operatives in the Empire have never found any record of this offshoot civilization, the chances are good that the Vecka are intentionally hiding, possibly from Dalgir itself. We'll know more after we have solved a problem that has come up."

"Problem?"

"For the time being, we've been forced to cease our efforts to question the girl. You saw how agitated she became when memories of her brother surfaced. As a precaution I have stopped the interviews until an approach safer than narcoquiz can be worked out. The information she carries is far too valuable to risk damaging her needlessly."

I shuddered a bit at the thought of Felira fighting narcoquiz. Other methods of extracting information from a human mind exist—methods that are standard procedure among the Dalgiri. Mostly they leave the victim a drooling vegetable. The Confederation occasionally resorted to such methods, but only as a last resort. If it was a case of one person's well-being against that of two hundred billion, however . . .

"You aren't going to do anything dangerous or painful to her, are you?"

Jouniel smiled. "That depends on how good a conversationalist you are."

"Me? What have I got to do with it?"

"Dal has taken the liberty of requesting that the young lady have dinner with you this evening. She has accepted. You will very gently work the conversation around to the information we must have to mount our expedition to her timeline."

"Why me?"

Jouniel didn't answer. Instead, a familiar voice echoed through the conference room from behind me: "Because you lucky S.O.B., the girl seems to be in love with you!"

I turned to face Dal Corst, who was lounging just inside the door, a smile splitting his face from ear to ear.

"Not 'love,' " Jouniel corrected. "More like an infatuation—possibly just an emotional dependence."

"I don't get it," I said. "We were only together for a few bora, and all I did was try to keep her mind off her brother. Hell, we were in our vacsuits. It's hard to strike up a romance while covered from head to toe in three inches of rubber."

"It isn't very complex, Watchman. The girl recently spent several days under extreme mental strain. There was the emotional stress of her escape, followed by pursuit across a number of timelines. Then came the fight on the Moon, her brother's injury, and their trek to the cave. By that time, she had resigned herself to death. When you found her, you offered her life instead. In such a situation the subconscious has trouble distinguishing between relief and romance, especially if the object of that relief is from a far-off land, and a member of the opposite sex.

"By now, she has inflated you to about ten times life-size. You are her anchor to reality, her defense against the ugly truths around her. You will have to be very careful about living up to that image."

I sat for a minute and thought about the problem. Somehow Jouniel's explanation still didn't seem reasonable. I cleared my throat and turned to Dal. "I see what you meant in the aircar. It does look like I have a fairy godmother, doesn't it?"

"Amen, brother."

CHAPTER 15

I had my last case of blind-date nerves when I was eighteen and took the prettiest girl in my class to the high school prom. You know the feeling—clammy hands, dry mouth, the worry you are going to say something wrong and embarrass the girl or yourself. Luckily, it's something that disappears with age . . . like pimples.

It does, huh?

If so, my mental state for the rest of the day was an omen that I was about to develop a terminal case of acne.

By the time I buzzed Felira's room in Headquarters Medical Center, I had the butterflies in my stomach pretty well under control. But my first sight of her as the door hissed open was enough to grow a whole new crop.

She was dressed in an evening gown of the latest Jaftan style, a wisp of blue gauze that did little to conceal an athletic, rounded figure while allowing intermittent tantalizing glimpses of those few patches of flesh it did cover. Felira's eyes peered through an unfamiliar floral pattern and her hair fell to her shoulders in a silky waterfall of midnight softness.

In the span of time between two heartbeats, I decided I liked the effect.

"Hi, remember me?" was the extent of suave I could dredge up on the spur of the moment.

Her smile came up like a new sunrise at the same moment I got my first whiff of her perfume. My knees turned to rubber.

"How could I forget the hero who rescued me from certain death, Watchman?"

"I just wish I could have done more to help your brother. And the name's Duncan, remember?"

"Clan Rossa and I thank you for what you tried to do . . . Duncan."

"You honor me."

"The honor is mine."

"Are you hungry?"

"Famished."

"Then we'll be off, milady. Our chariot awaits without."

"But I cannot!"

"Why not?"

Felira blushed, not easy with a complexion as dark as hers. "An unmarried woman of Syllsin does not appear in public clad so. I would shame my sept and family."

"Nonsense, that dress conforms to all local codes, ordinances, usages, traditions, mores, and customs. Besides, you are beautiful in it."

"The truth? No one will stare?"

"The truth." I took her hands in mine. "As for staring, can you blame anyone for wanting to look upon such a vision?"

She smiled and seemed to put her embarrassment out of mind. "In that case, let us proceed," she said, fastening a matching cloak over the gown. "I'm so hungry I could eat a Veckan tax collector without salt."

"Good," I said. "I know a restaurant where Veckan tax collectors are the house specialty."

In the mountains above Jafta, the restaurant was laid out to resemble an open-air garden. Its polarized dome managed to show off the carpet of city lights below without washing out the stars above. The dome interior was a jungle of fragrant plants, with each table placed for maximum privacy, in its own alcove.

Felira was entranced.

After a while, she relaxed a bit. It was during my efforts at translating the menu that I heard her truly laugh for the first time.

"Here's a good one," I said. " 'A tantalizing repast of boiled monkey eyes in a delicious sauce of raw entrails from overripe fish.' "

That was when she laughed. "Sounds delicious," she said.

I chuckled too, my own mood lightening considerably. It was as if an invisible wall between us had been lifted.

All through dinner we talked of our homes—me of what it was like to grow up in the U.S., she alternating with anecdotes of a childhood on Syllsin. I was a bit surprised that even with the Veckan jackboot on their necks, Syllsintaag children grew up happy and carefree. Of course, children have always had that talent regardless of the indignities their elders manage to perpetrate on each other.

As the evening wore on and Felira became more comfortable, I gently nudged the conversation in the way Jouniel wanted. Finally, the subject touched on the Vecka and I energized the recorder in my pocket, feeling an irrational pang of guilt as I did so.

"To tell the truth, I barely noticed the Vecka until I was fourteen," Felira said. "Until then the War Masters were just a story mothers punished their children with . . . like the Cave Trolls or the Old Man of the Swamp. Oh, and once when my father took me to Rossa-Home on business, one of the tithemasters passed us on the mall. I remember the smell of him even from nearly thirty *eppa* downwind."

"They don't station troops in your cities?" I asked, mildly surprised. I had been thinking Syllsin must be akin to what the Netherlands or Norway were like during the Nazi occupation.

"They wouldn't dare!" Felira said, fire returning briefly to her eyes. "We outnumber them a hundred to one and would overwhelm them. No, the Vecka rule by threat of mass destruction alone, and keep to themselves otherwise."

"Doesn't anyone ever revolt?"

"There was a revolt among the fishermen of South Rana about twenty years ago. The ruins are still unsafe to enter."

"What happened when you were fourteen?" For a second I thought I had committed a *faux pas* as her face clouded up and her gaze refused to meet mine. Instead she self-consciously pushed an unidentifiable piece of seafood around her plate with a utensil that looked something like a fork.

When she spoke, it was with new hesitancy. "That was the year the press gangs took Graf for the technical schools on Veck. I never expected to see him again."

"Then how? . . ."

"I was taken hostage. Our district had shown some unrest and the Governor demanded the presence of sons and daughters of Clan leaders to insure our good conduct. We were interned at Brolis Base, where I was put to work in the kitchens. It was there that I found Graf. He planned to steal a ship and escape to the wilderness. He had nearly completed his preparations when we found each other."

"Preparations?" I asked. "What kind?"

"Oh, many things. Like stealing a hypnodisk used to train pilots and implanting himself with the necessary skills. He had become friendly with some of the Veckans' serfs—descendants of those captured in raids—who guarded us. He was also very good at fooling the base computers to get equipment he needed."

"How did you manage to steal the ship? Wouldn't they guard their warships more closely than their gold?"

Felira gave a humorless laugh. "We have a saying on Syllsin: 'The truth cannot be too many times spoken.' Normally we Syllsintaag are not allowed near the great ships. The crews are made up solely of Vecka and their serfs. We 'wild men' aren't to be trusted.

"No, our chance was the result of good fortune. I had been at Brolis Base a year when rumors began about the new alliance with the Dalgiri. That was midwinter. By spring the number of Veckan warships based at Brolis had nearly doubled. One morning, a strange fleet appeared in the sky over the base. Some of the serfs wailed that we were being attacked. But the Veckan ships rose to join them and the whole armada flew off to the north."

"Any idea where they went?"

"One of the cleaning women overheard an officer speak of Manifest Destiny and the beginnings of a new Empire, whatever that meant."

"So you and your brother took advantage of their absence to escape?"

"Oh no! The soldiers were as watchful as ever. It was

later, during the confusion, that we found our opportunity."

"Confusion?"

"Only two ships of twenty-three returned, both small Dalgiri vessels. Not a single Veckan warcraft survived. Graf and I were in the work party that offloaded the wounded. We hid in a supply locker until just before dawn. Then we overpowered the single guard aboard, and raced for the mountains. We were unlucky. The other ship must have been crewed because it gave chase immediately. We were forced to seek the time gate on the Moon and flee. They pursued us and we fled again. We jumped blindly until we found ourselves trapped in a universe without exit. We hid in a crater and when our pursuers came into view, we attacked them. We were lucky. We won."

"And the next thing you knew, I jumped out of nowhere at you and scared you to death, right?" I asked, trying to lighten the mood.

"I thought the Moon uninhabited in that universe. We only fled the ship because Graf wasn't sure he had destroyed our tormentors. I had resigned myself to waiting in the cave until my oxygen ran out. Believe me, after the first moment of fear, I was very glad to see you, Duncan."

I bit my lip and mulled over what I had learned. Apparently there were at least three temporal portals on the Syllsin timeline. One connected Syllsin to Veck, one connected Syllsin to wherever it was that the Dalgiri had raided, and one connected Syllsin's Moon with Europo-American's Moon through a long, arduous series of transitions.

"Curiouser and curiouser," I muttered to myself.

"What?" Felira asked, puzzled.

I smiled. "Just something we say at home when we don't understand something," I said. Then I hesitated, not sure how to broach the next subject.

"How would you like to go home?"

She was stunned for a moment, her wineglass hovering midway between the table and her lips. "That . . . isn't . . . possible . . . is it? We jumped blindly. I could not tell you where Syllsin is even if I were a pilot."

"No problem there. We have the jump recorder from

your ship. We will be able to backtrack from that." I hurriedly sketched our need to find out what secrets in addition to the teleportation generator the Dalgiri might have learned from Veck. I didn't mention that she had just given Talador an even more critical problem. The Dalgiri had launched a major expedition into Paratime somewhere beyond Syllsin. They limped home with their tails between their legs. Anyone who could give the Empire that bloody a nose was someone who needed watching. I finished up by repeating my question.

"Would you like us to take you home?"

"More than anything!" she squealed, throwing her arms around my neck. I sat back and enjoyed it, my nose buried in perfumed hair, my skin keenly aware of the warm, soft femininity pressed against it. Finally, she released me.

"When do we start?"

"We start planning for the mission tomorrow morning. We launch in a quarter year at the latest."

The expedition to Syllsin didn't get started in three months as planned. It was more like three days.

When Felira and I returned to her room, I found a message from Hral Ssaroth, Dal's deputy, waiting for me. I said my good-byes and hotfooted it the half-mile to the Headquarters Complex Operations Center, where I found a state of near-panic.

"Hi, what's up?" I asked after I'd waited for Ssaroth to finish with the three people ahead of me in line.

"Where the hell have you been?" he growled.

"Out getting the information Dal wanted from Felira."

His face clouded and I thought he was about to explode when he caught himself and grinned. "Sorry. Things haven't gone well for me today. Here, take this over to one of those empty desks and study it."

"This" was a record cube for a standard screen reader. It didn't take long to figure out what had gotten everyone into such a tizzy.

The cube contained the analysis of the downed shuttle's trip recorder. Felira and Graf Transtas had passed through eleven timelines making good their escape. And if the number of transitions was surprising, the identification of the portals involved was even more so. Except for their first jump from Syllsin's Moon, every gateway used was in a universe already in the Taladoran Paratime catalogs. None of the portals was of prime quality. Some were open for no more than a few months at a time. Others held for a decade or more, then went dormant for centuries.

The bottom line was that the most direct path from Talador to Syllsin would be unusable in less than a month. The last portal in the series, the one on Syllsin's moon, would close in twenty-nine days. When it next reopened, in a few months, three others in the series would be inactive. The highway between Felira's universe and Europo-American would be closed.

"Well, did you read the bad news?" Ssaroth asked after I'd returned the record cube to his desk.

I nodded. "Reminds me of launching a grand-tour mission of the outer planets. You either go during the few months your launch window is open or you don't go at all."

Ssaroth snorted his agreement. "Dal figures our 'launch window' closes no more than one Tenday from this morning."

"Where is the boss, anyway?"

"Out begging for ships."

"Any chance of finding an alternate series of portals?" I asked.

"There's always a chance of that. The Paratime interconnectivity in that region is quite high."

"Can we be ready in time?"

"We have no choice. The fleet leaves in three hundred bora, ready or not."

"Anything I can do to help?"

"Find a desk and plug into the computer net. There are a million things to do between now and the time we ship out. Now go away and don't bother me, I'm busy."

"Temporal transition in thirty centibora. All crewmen to transition stations, all weapons crews to battle stations. Thirty and counting!"

The great bulk of Taladoran dreadnought *City of Isvall* hummed around me as the annunciator echoed to the "transition stations" call. I was seated in a compartment that was a smaller version of the Combat Control Center in the lunar fortresses.

Soufilcar Jouniel sat at the master control board on a raised platform in the center of a circle of consoles. I sat in one of the two observer's stations directly behind her. Felira sat in the other. As the chronometers blinked down to zero and Jouniel directed her technicians in a calm, unhurried voice, Felira's hand sought mine for reassurance.

I was glad it did. I needed a bit of reassurance about then.

The bulkhead speakers came alive once more: *"Twenty centibora."*

On screens around us floated the hulking forms of the other three vessels of our fleet. To my right was *City of Ool,* another dreadnought of the *Isvall's* class. She was a huge spheroid covered with raised housings, weapons blisters, and radiator fins to cool the great fusion generators that powered her. Our two other ships were *Kreshni* and *Zirca,* cruiser class shuttles whose silhouettes were that of a blunt cylinder with rounded ends. The backdrop for each ship was the familiar dull gray of a lunar landscape.

"Weapons to full standby power. Transition in ten centibora."

"Look alive," Jouniel called out to her technicians. "I want a full sensor sweep the instant we exit the portal on the other side."

"Transition!"

The screens around us flashed once as our fleet disappeared and a new world appeared in our sky. There was a flurry of activity around me as our long-range sensors began to scan for signs of hostile activity. I held my breath, waiting for the inevitable moment when we would be discovered.

While we waited, all eyes gravitated toward the main screen. Centered in it was the familiar blue-white bowling ball that I had gazed upon so often in the last couple of years. Here and there patches of brownish green peeked from under clouds, adding variety to the scene.

My inspection of the new world was interrupted by Dal Corst's voice issuing from the annunciator speaker.

"Is Felira there?"

"I'm here."

"Where is Brolis Base located with respect to us?"

"I'm not sure. Let me get oriented. There's Gassilrow, and Sfarble, and the Islands of Rem almost directly in the center of the screen," she said aloud, verbalizing her thoughts. "Brolis is on the other side of the planet."

"You and Duncan report to me immediately. I'm calling in the rest of the fleet and we'll get you on your way before we go into hiding. Jouniel, turn over your command to your deputy and join us as well."

"We're on our way."

CHAPTER 16

THE Contact Team would number four, that being the minimum number who could do the job and still have a reasonable chance of escaping detection. The four people chosen were Felira, Jouniel, Hral Ssaroth, and me. Jouniel would be in command and handle any diplomatic haggling that might arise. Ssaroth would be her assistant. He had not been on the original roster but was added when he pointed out that an expert in cloak-and-dagger work could prove invaluable if something went wrong. Having someone who could impersonate a Veck was another factor in his favor.

Felira would guide us and act as our liaison with the Clan Leaders. No one expected her to act against the interests of her people, but she had made it clear she considered herself in our debt and would protect our interests as well.

And me? My job was to assist Jouniel and Ssaroth in any way possible and to provide a strong back where needed. Unofficially, of course, I was along to provide Felira a reason for remaining loyal to us and to act in my usual capacity as rabbit's foot.

We made the jump from Syllsin's moon to the surface in a courier shuttle, one of dead *Concorde*'s class. Our arrival in enemy territory was punctuated by the usual thunderclap of displaced air and a stomach-wrenching six-hundred-percent increase in the g-field around us. Even braced for it, I found myself gasping for breath long minutes afterward.

We materialized at local midnight in one of the larger wildernesses. When we were fairly sure that our arrival had gone undetected, our pilot lost no time in racing for Transtas Keep, Felira's hometown.

The four-hour flight was the wildest of my life. The pilot hugged every hill and valley across an entire continent. After the first hour I didn't need to look to see the bruises on my chest and thighs where the safety straps cut deeply into me. More than once I found myself wishing the equations of teleportation allowed point-to-point travel on the Earth. My bruised hide was fast becoming a monument to the inviolability of the laws of physics.

Well before first light we found ourselves in a wooded area near a highway leading to Transtas Keep. After unloading us and our equipment, the shuttle rose to treetop level and silently whooshed off in the direction of the nearest ocean. The crew had orders to head well out to sea before making the jump back to the fleet on the Moon.

We were dressed in what Felira assured us were authentic replicas of Syllsintaag hunting garb. Our equipment was contained in four packs that matched the green camouflage outfits, with Ssaroth's and mine being twice the size of the women's (thus the need for strong backs). Our weapons were slug-throwing rifles so familiar that it made me a bit homesick to cradle one in my arms.

After the shuttle had disappeared into the night, we waited until it was light enough to see and then struck out for a road five miles away through thick forest. I quickly discovered that two years of low gravity and desk jobs had ruined my stamina. After half a mile or so, however, I got my second wind and began to take an interest in my surroundings.

It quickly became evident that Syllsin was an exception to the rule that species tend to be replicated across Paratime. Whatever the mechanism that seeds the timelines with life forms, it was out of kilter here. The trees were mostly giant ferns of a sort I had never seen before. The animals were different, too. A quick glimpse of the avian life left me convinced that I had seen a feathered pterodactyl. Brief encounters with small carnivorous flowers, twin-tailed almost-monkeys that whistled when frightened, and something that might have been a storybook gnome if not for its obvious snout and paws, left me with the impression that I had fallen into an intergalactic zoo.

Felira seemed perfectly at home amid the odd life of the forest, so I concluded all this must be normal. I filed the information away under the "strange things witnessed in the course of a lifetime" category in my mind, and promptly forgot about it.

The road we sought turned out to be a conventional blacktop highway. We walked beside it for almost two miles until we came to a featureless metal kiosk. Felira eased off her pack with a sigh and stepped up to the structure, opening a plate in its side to reveal a flush-mounted television screen.

Felira performed an unfamiliar ritual—the equivalent of dialing, I presumed—and after a few moments the screen cleared to reveal a bearded man.

Within seconds both parties to the conversation had great streams of tears rolling down their cheeks as they chattered away in Syllsintaag. Soon the screen went dead and Felira turned to join us, suggesting that we pull back into the woods. "Father is sending Uncle Mors for us. We are to wait out of sight."

"What did you tell your father about us?" Jouniel asked.

"Nothing. I told him I was coming home and that I was bringing three friends who had helped me."

Forty minutes later a small hover truck—something like an air-cushion vehicle supported by a force field—pulled up to the kiosk and a short, stocky man got out. I watched through electronic binoculars as the newcomer scanned the surrounding woods. After half a minute, he raised fingers to lips and let loose a piercing, ululating whistle.

"Uncle Mors!" Felira yelled, and raced down to the man beside the car.

"Better wait a few centibora before going down, Hral. Wouldn't want our man to mistake you for a Veck."

"Right," Ssaroth said. "I'll wait for your signal."

Jouniel and I followed slowly behind Felira, to allow them their private moment of homecoming, and to keep a wary eye all around.

We rode to Transtas Keep in the back of the hover truck, a repair vehicle to judge from the tools and parts arrayed in the bins that lined the van's sloping sides. A close examination of a few of the "spare parts" left me with an uneasy feeling. It looked as if Syllsintaag science had advanced on a wide front before the Veckan invasion. Just how wide that front had been was a question of immediate and vital interest.

The machine that would provide us with the answer lay in the bottom of my pack inside a gray case the size of a child's lunch box. In that small volume was packed an electronic ferret, an information thief designed to probe the large computer nets every major Paratime civilization relied on.

I had scoffed when Dal first showed it to me.

"What, this dinky little thing is going to crack the Veckan master computer banks?"

He had chuckled. "That 'dinky little thing' is the product of over two thousand years of computer science. We began its development about the time Pythagoras began drawing figures in the dirt."

"Oh," I said, thinking about the computer revolution at home. I tried to imagine that same mad scramble of invention after a couple of millennia and gave it up. My mind's "boggle threshold" is too low.

Felira's father met us at the door of her home, a block-long structure that reminded me more of an apartment building than a house. The elder Transtas gave a single cry of joy at the sight of his daughter, sweeping her into a massive bear hug. Jouniel, Ssaroth, and I hung back as we had at the kiosk while the inevitable crying and welcomes subsided. When he finally released her, he turned to us and bowed, greeting us in Syllsintaag.

"I'm sorry, but I don't speak your language," I said in Dalgiri.

His eyebrows shot up at the same time he caught sight of Hral Ssaroth's *Neanderthaloid* features. He turned to his daughter and spat a quick sentence in Syllsintaag.

Felira responded in the same tongue before switching to Dalgiri. "Father, I have the honor to introduce Soufilcar Jouniel, Duncan MacElroy, and Hral Ssaroth, emissaries of the Taladoran Confederation, a great nation beyond Time. I ask that they be given all the courtesies of guests in this, our home. Duncan, Hral, Jouniel, may I present Grafftar Bax Transtas, Hereditary Lawgiver of Transtas Sept, Clan Rossa. My father."

Bax Transtas gave his daughter a quizzical look and intoned what was obviously a formula of welcome. Jouniel then recited a little speech that Felira had written, saying that as good guests we would defend the household as if it were our own.

Transtas completed the ritual with a final bow then straightened up and turned to Felira. "I have done as you requested, daughter. Perhaps you will now explain what is happening here?"

Felira begged off by pleading fatigue from our long journey and the need to discuss a family matter of the gravest importance. Bax Transtas agreed to Felira's request, and in a few minutes Jouniel, Ssaroth, and I were being ushered to meet the rest of the family.

If the house seemed large on the outside, it was cavernous from within. Four wings, each three stories high, surrounded a central courtyard filled with green, growing things and a small fountain. A score of people ranging in age from eight months to eighty years were gathered around the fountain. We were introduced to each in turn.

Besides her mother and father, Felira's sister, uncle, and their assorted families lived in the house. These, it was explained, were only the *immediate* family. Apparently just about everybody in town could claim a distant blood relationship. Being a member of a clan other than Clan Rossa in Transtas Keep was akin to being a non-Mormon in Salt Lake City.

After the introductions were over, Felira's mother showed us to our rooms on the uppermost floor of the house. After assuring herself that we were comfortably settled, she made her apologies and withdrew. The only other person we saw that day was the young girl who brought us lunch and dinner.

Between meals we loafed, talked, and played three-handed card games with a Syllsintaag deck I found in my room. Occasionally we would hear sonorous chanting from somewhere below, and once a curiously flat music could be heard through the open door. Shortly after dark, Jouniel said goodnight and retired to her room. Ssaroth and I talked a couple of hours more before he too took his leave. I lay down in my bed and was asleep in seconds.

The next thing I knew, a small hand was shaking me awake, and its owner—a cherubic little girl of six—told me in broken Dalgiri that breakfast was being served in the main courtyard. After a quick shower and shave, I made my way to the lift.

The family was already seated at the table, laughing and talking as if nothing had happened the day before. I took an empty chair across from Felira and on her father's right.

"Good morning, sleepyhead," Felira said, laughing. "Are you hungry?"

"Famished. Why didn't someone wake me earlier?"

"I looked in on you," Jouniel said from two places down the table on the other side. "You were dead to the world. That hike must have really tired you out."

"I hope you will understand about yesterday," Felira's father said, passing me a bowl of fruit. "We of Syllsin mourn our dead in private."

"I understand, Grafftar."

" 'Grafftar' is a title. In this vile language we are speaking, I would be called 'Judge.' My friends call me Bax."

"I'm Duncan."

"I know who you are, young man. My daughter has had much to say on the subject."

Ssaroth chuckled from his place across from Jouniel as he split a squab in two with greasy fingers. "It will be interesting to see if the flesh-and-blood version can live up to the fictional account."

I pretended I didn't hear him, and dug into breakfast. I would have been more convincing if the family hadn't broken into hysterics at Ssaroth's lame joke.

After breakfast, Bax Transtas led us to his library.

"Shall we get down to business?" he asked, suddenly sharp-eyed and suspicious. "My second daughter tells me I owe you people a debt. How much is it going to cost me?"

"Has Felira explained who we are and where we come from?" Jouniel asked.

"Yes," he said, eying Ssaroth. "Although I still have

difficulty accepting that a Veck can be other than a Veck."

"We assure you, Grafftar, that your daughter has spoken the literal truth about us." Jouniel hesitated a moment before launching into an abbreviated history of the Taladoran-Dalgiri War and a recounting of our discovery that the Near Men had the teleportation generator.

She finished with: "To be blunt, Grafftar, we are here to discover what else our enemies may have learned from your masters. We cannot again allow ourselves to be caught so thoroughly by surprise."

"And you wish us to help you attach this—ferret, did you call it?—to a stronghold information bank?"

"Yes, Grafftar."

"Are you willing to help us in return?"

"We cannot," Ssaroth said. "Our time here is limited. Perhaps in the future when we have charted a secure path between your world and our own . . ."

Bax looked pensively into an unlit fireplace, hesitating some while before speaking. When he finally broke silence, it was with a tone of deep regret:

"I owe you my daughter's life, a debt that cannot easily be repaid. Yet you ask a great deal. Do you expect us to attack the Governor's Stronghold itself? If so, I must tell you my daughter's life, as dear as it is to me, is not worth it. Such an assault would cost us thousands of lives at the very least."

"If need be, Grafftar, we can call down our fleet and use it against any installation you name. Your people need not take an active part."

"And after you have left? Do you think the War Masters will not suspect that we had a hand in it? No, I do not have the power to rule on this. I will have to place it before the Revolutionary Committee. In the meantime, I think I had best hide you three and Felira. This is a small town and tongues will wag."

Dinner that night was a private affair. Jouniel, Ssaroth, and I dined with Felira and her parents in their apartments. Afterward, we were hustled out a back door to the same hover truck we had arrived in. Well past midnight, we finally arrived at our destination, a farm in the middle of a vast wilderness.

*   *   *

Life on the farm took on a simple routine while we waited for word from the Revolutionary Committee. Up with the—for want of a better species—chickens, Felira and I helped the owner and his wife with their chores while Jouniel pored over a stack of Veckan history books Bax Transtas had given her, and Hral Ssaroth spent his time brooding.

In the afternoons, we hiked the surrounding forest and tried to forget the deadline that was bearing down on us. One afternoon we were exploring the territory to the north for the first time. I wore tattered shorts, hiking boots, and a backpack. Felira was similarly attired, with the addition of a sleeveless blouse of light cotton whose tails she tied in a knot at her midriff. We had invited Jouniel along, but as usual, she pleaded the press of work.

I was beginning to worry about Jouniel. She pored over her small library day and night because something about Syllsin vexed her. Whatever it was, solving the mystery had become an obsession with her. She would halt her researches only for the two hours each day that she and Ssaroth spent conferring with Dal Corst. The subject of these conferences was always the same: What to do if the Revolutionary Committee delayed much longer?

Time was running out.

It was now T minus 120 hours and counting—just five days before the long chain of portals back to Europo-American and Talador would be broken.

Not that the "marooning" would have to be permanent. We knew of an alternative series of transitions that would get us home—the path through time the Dalgiri used to travel to Veck. But four ships can no more fight Dalgir than a moth can fly in the face of a hurricane. So if we delayed longer than five days, we would be stuck until we were able to scout out a brand-new transition series—assuming one existed.

So while I enjoyed myself with Felira, Jouniel held frenzied negotiations with Dal, and Ssaroth refereed. Under discussion were the date and time when *City of Isvall* would stir from her resting place and take matters into her own hands. If the Syllsintaag delayed too long, the tacticians aboard the flagship planned to raid a stronghold, hook into its computer net, suck it dry, and escape through the Lunar portal before the opposition could organize. The only problems with such a plan were that: (a) it would betray Felira's people and leave them to suffer the Veckan revenge alone; (b) it would require flattening Brolis Base with nuclear weapons, thereby killing the million or so innocents who lived around the base; and (c) it might not work.

Jouniel wasn't the only one who had seemed distracted lately. Felira had been unnaturally quiet for the previous week. I thought I knew what was bothering her, and decided to bring it out in the open.

"You know, of course, that we are going to have to do something soon, don't you?" I asked as we sat beneath a giant fern and rested.

She looked at me with troubled eyes and sighed. "I know. Jouniel speaks a great deal to that little radio of hers. It isn't hard to guess what is being said."

"Is there anything you can do to convince your father and his friends of the seriousness of the situation?"

"I have tried," she said, tears welling in her eyes. "I report to Father every day by the courier who brings Jouniel and Ssaroth messages, just as they report to your higher authorities on the Moon."

"And?"

"The sentiment in Committee is against us. I fear that they will forbid the Clans to help you."

"You know what that means."

"That the fleet will take independent action and there will be war again on this world."

I nodded. "Unless we can stop them."

We sat in silence for a long time. After one of those eternities that pass in a few seconds, I leaned over and kissed her. She returned my embrace eagerly. After a longer while, we broke for air and I sat back to think.

"We've got to do something," I said.

"But what—" Felira froze in midsentence and glanced skyward.

"What's the matter?" I asked, my voice a harsh whisper.

"Aircraft, don't you hear it?"

I cocked my head to listen. She was right. "Veckan?"

"No. Their aircars are silent. This sounds like one of ours."

We crouched and listened as the buzzing grew louder. Suddenly, the plane passed over us and arrowed straight toward the farm. Felira relaxed when she caught sight of it.

"It's all right. That is a courier craft for the Committee. They must have come to a decision."

We jogged all the way back to the farm. Jouniel and Bax Transtas met us at the door. Jouniel had a twinkle in her eye.

"What's up?" I asked.

"Get into your best clothes and pack the ferret. We are going to a party."

"A what?"

"A party. We have been invited to drinks and dinner by the District Governor himself."

"*What?*"

"Come on now, we don't want to be late."

Bax Transtas briefed us on the situation as we flew northwest toward Rossa-Home, the major Syllsintaag city, seat of the largest of the extended clans, and site of the local Veckan stronghold.

As Jouniel had surmised, the Revolutionary Committee had quickly divided into two camps. One had welcomed the opportunity to help us, while the other could see no good from our presence on their world. The sessions had turned into a bitter fight between those who saw the Taladoran presence as a chance to gain a powerful ally and those who liked change even less than the status quo.

Bax Transtas, on the strength of his daughter's reports, had led our proponents. Every time the debate threatened to go off track, he hauled it back again, pointedly noting that time was running out and the ships on the Moon would not wait forever. Finally, when everyone was exhausted, he and a few like-minded members worked out a scheme to satisfy all.

The plan called on us to get help from an unlikely source, the Rossa-Home District Governor.

Like many conquerors throughout history, the Vecka had grown soft from easy living. They were the War

Masters of old in name only, leaning ever more heavily on their serfs and servants for the day-to-day supervision of their dominion.

The District Governors were the landed gentry of Syllsin feudal society. After a century of revolts, assassinations, and riots, most had learned to stay in their fortresses and were content if the taxes were collected on time and the press gangs made their quotas for the technical schools on Veck.

Baron Ylgost 't Prasilwant was Governor at Rossa-Home Stronghold. The Baron had recently sent word to the Council of Clans that he would be entertaining an important dignitary for the feast of *Baedroph* this year, and that the usual roster of Clan Leaders and their ladies would be expected to attend.

It was Bax's plan to smuggle Jouniel and me into the stronghold as members of the Syllsintaag delegation. Ssaroth would bring the ferret later, entering the fortress openly as a Veck. Once inside, we would wait until we could slip away unnoticed then tap the ferret into the stronghold computers. With luck, we would have the information we needed and quickly be gone with the Vecka none the wiser.

I had to admit Bax's idea was better than any we had thought up and more subtle than the battering-ram approach *Isvall*'s staff had been urging on Dal Corst.

CHAPTER 17

WE arrived in Rossa-Home City just as the sun dropped below the horizon and painted the sky in reds, yellows, and golds. Bax had a hovercar whisk us to a block of row houses near the center of the city. Inside, we found a delegation from the Revolutionary Committee awaiting us.

After the formal introductions, Jouniel and Felira were ushered upstairs to a makeup artist. As far as Jouniel was concerned, we had no choice. She *had* to be disguised. No one would ever mistake her for a native. Felira, on the other hand, was going under the brush in case someone recognized her and knew of the missing Dalgiri shuttle.

The Syllsintaag conspirators debated disguising me as well, and decided against it. My looks were fairly close to local norms, especially since my hikes with Felira had left me deeply tanned. Bax judged the risk of wearing my own face to be less than if I wore makeup.

As the two women were being worked on, Bax led Ssaroth and me upstairs to a back room on the third floor. I gasped as I glanced out the window. The safe house fronted an immense plaza a mile on a side in the center of the city. The square was devoid of any obstruction, save for a squat fortress with sloping armor-plate sides, the walls of which glowed blood-red in the dusk light.

I studied the fortress with my binoculars. The building was featureless save for a row of gunports near the top of the walls. The only other opening was a tall gate at the base of the nearer rampart.

"Rossa-Home Stronghold," Bax said. "Study it carefully. Afterward we will examine sketches of the interior and maps showing the computer rooms."

I was still scanning the fortress when Jouniel joined us. She had been so completely transformed into a Syllsintaag matron that I didn't recognize her at first. She moved to the window and stared at the stronghold.

"Big, isn't it?"

"Bigger than I expected," I agreed, nodding.

"See anything interesting?"

"Look at the aircar," I said, speaking in Taladoran. I pointed to the patrol vehicle I had watched circle the fortress ramparts for the last ten minutes.

Jouniel took the binoculars and studied the car in the growing gloom. After a minute or so, she lowered the glasses and turned to me with a quizzical look on her face.

"So?"

"How long since the Vecka left the Dalgiri Empire?"

"About three hundred years."

"If that aircar is a three-hundred-year-old model, I'll eat it."

She studied the car at length this time, pursing her lips in concentration. "An interesting thought, especially in light of a few discrepancies I have noted."

"Such as?"

"The Veckan tongue, as it is spoken by our friends here —it doesn't jibe with the notion of a three-century-old colony from the Dalgiri Empire, either. It's too modern by far."

"Too modern?" I asked.

"It has too many of the structures and usages of the modern Dalgiri tongue. When first assigned Felira's case, I thought I would clear up the mystery of Veckan origin by linguistic analysis alone. But the computer refused to interpolate the data—very frustrating, considering the size of the data base."

"Come now, Jouniel," Ssaroth said, laughing. "Your programming must have an error in it. Linguistic analysis is usually foolproof."

"You would think so," she said, suddenly switching back to Syllsintaag. "I beg your indulgence, Grafftar. My colleagues and I were discussing some technical details concerning that patrol vehicle, for which we lack the proper vocabulary in the Veckan language. Will you forgive our impoliteness?"

Bax didn't make an issue of it, but I suspect he wasn't fooled.

In another hour we had been thoroughly briefed and had studied a number of sketches and hand-drawn maps of the stronghold's interior. We were as ready as we would ever be.

Most of our fellow conspirators had already gone ahead, leaving in small groups of two or three. Each carried a gaily wrapped package, the token of esteem the Baron required from his guests to convince VIPs from Veck that all was well in the district.

For once the Syllsintaag were more than happy to go along with the charade. Ssaroth too would carry a gaily wrapped package into the fortress. His was rectangular, about the size of a child's lunch box.

"Ah, the Lawgiver of Clan Rossa, welcome to my home!"

The speaker was an obscenely fat man with overhanging eye ridges and misshapen teeth. He was dressed in a badly cut dark uniform, with a holster and an ornate dagger hanging from a tooled leather belt. Bax acknowledged his greeting with a deep bow.

"Greetings, Excellency. I hope all is well with your family."

"Well enough, Grafftar Transtas, well enough. Except for my youngest, Cephiel. I don't know what I am going to do with that boy if he doesn't stop getting involved with the native girls. But then, your wenches do enjoy the attentions of our young men, do they not?"

The Governor's voice was one that carried. He didn't seem to notice the sudden stiffening of Syllsintaag spines throughout the large hall. If Bax felt the same urge to throttle him everyone else seemed to, he didn't show it.

"Excellency, I would like to introduce my cousin and her family—Mullarow Transtas; her son, Vrieler; his wife, Harla . . ." We each kissed the Veck's outstretched palm as we were introduced. (Felira was right. They do stink.)

". . . Mullarow, this is our host, Baron Ylgost 't Prasil-want."

Jouniel went into her giggling-matron act while I did my best to project the image of a stupid, but honest lunk.

The Baron seemed to lap it up.

"You were always a good servant, Grafftar. I am mindful to grant you a boon. Name what you will."

"I have but a single wish, Excellency. My daughter is being held at Brolis Base. If you could intercede with the Governor of that district to have her returned to me . . ."

"Hmmph. If I return your child to you, others will besiege me with similar requests. I will have to think upon it."

"You are most kind, Excellency."

"Pardon me, children, but I must see to my guest of honor. Would that I could send a servant, but we don't want to offend the great man, now do we?" With that he waddled off into the crowd.

"What was that business about releasing Felira?" I asked, my voice just loud enough to carry the few inches to Bax's ear.

"I was testing to see if he had had any reports about the stolen shuttle."

"And?"

"Inconclusive. The Baron is a crafty old lizard and he could have been playing with me."

With that disturbing thought, we dropped back into character and began to circulate. Felira and I studiously avoided speaking to anyone we hadn't met in the safe house. Felira did most of the talking. I just stayed in character and gawked at my surroundings.

Someone had gone to a lot of trouble to remodel the utilitarian walls of the original fortress, constructing something in an architectural style that was a cross between Late Rococo and Early Parisian Whorehouse. Like the Governor's ill-fitting uniform, it merely heightened the feeling that the War Masters of old had fled this place.

A few late arrivals filtered in, including a half-dozen Vecka. These were treated with exaggerated respect by the second-class citizens present. Mostly the newcomers seemed bored with it all and quickly gravitated into their own little clump at one end of the room, where a floor-to-ceiling tapestry revealed the glorious history of Veck while hiding the gunports behind which a dozen household troops supervised the gathering.

An hour later a squeal sounded in my ear. I steered Felira to Bax and Jouniel, who were talking with two Revolutionary Committee members—a tall, lanky man named Potnir and a hulking wrestler-type named Noor. To the casual observer, our shift should have looked like the usual Brownian motion of a cocktail party.

"Ssaroth and the ferret are here," I reported.

"Then let us begin," Bax said, his lips barely moving behind the idiot's smile he had worn all evening. "Duncan, you start off."

"Good luck," Felira said, squeezing my hand. I wanted to kiss her, but settled for returning the squeeze. I turned on my heel and sauntered out the door as if I didn't have a care.

Ssaroth was in the curtained alcove we had chosen for rendezvous. He was dressed in the same style as the Baron, except for lack of weapons. Bax, Potnir, and Noor quickly joined us, and we set off single file, tiptoeing through deserted corridors toward the stronghold's administrative section.

Ssaroth was our point man in case we encountered anyone in the corridors. It would be his job to distract guards or civil servants long enough for Potnir and Noor to overpower them.

I licked dry lips and tried to forget my fear as we inched along deserted corridors. Twice we waited as Noor neutralized automatic sensors. Once we tiptoed past a lighted office that was occupied. Luckily for him, the servant inside remained hunched over a screen with his back to us while we slipped past his open door.

Finally, we arrived at the computer center only to find our way barred by a locked steel door. Noor tackled the job and we were inside within half a minute. Ssaroth waved the overhead lights on as soon as the door closed behind us, and I went to work with the ferret.

Installing a ferret is simply a matter of removing an inspection cover or two from the host machine, tracing cables, and then making a few quick connections with inductive pickups.

As I traced cables I began to notice details of the terminal's construction and was immediately overcome by the same feeling I had had watching the aircar circle the ramparts earlier. The more I looked, the harder it was to shake the conviction that this particular machine was more advanced than current Dalgiri models.

Which was stupid. When the Vecka had left the Empire, Dalgiri computer science had been only slightly more advanced than that of modern-day Europo-American. I attributed my suspicions to a bad case of nerves and got back to work.

After five minutes of cable tracing, I had the ferret hooked up and energized. Now all that was necessary was to sit and wait for it to do its job. Thirty minutes passed very slowly, and I began, to wonder if something had gone wrong, but I didn't have time to pursue the thought. Suddenly voices were at the door!

Potnir quickly switched off the overhead light, and we sat in the dark holding our breaths, praying that whoever was outside would go away. No such luck. The door snicked open, spilling a long rectangle of corridor light across the floor. I shrank into the shadows as far as I could, crouching over the flickering lights of the ferret to shield them with my body.

The door snicked shut again, but not before two Neanderthal silhouettes stepped inside. Then came a series of Dalgir curses as a familiar voice searched for the light control.

The lights blazed on and things began to happen so quickly that it took minutes afterward to unscramble them in my mind.

The sudden radiance caught Baron Ylgost open-mouthed. His companion must have been equally shocked at discovering the supposedly empty room full of men, but he masked it better. That didn't surprise me, for the Baron's companion was no Veck.

Just by the way the hair on the back of my neck stood on end, I could tell I was facing a Dalgir. A Dalgir is to a Veck what Hitler was to Mussolini.

We were all frozen in our tracks for an instant before chaos broke loose.

Ylgost screamed and reached for his holstered pistol at

the same moment the Dalgir spat two words and grabbed for an inside pocket of his chemise.

Both were milliseconds too late as five bodies converged on where they stood.

Bax, Ssaroth, and I arrived more or less simultaneously at the Dalgir's position while Potnir and Noor concentrated on the Baron. Unfortunately, I arrived a bit ahead of the others and encountered a rapidly rising elbow full in the face.

After that I don't remember much about the fight except that the explosion of the Baron's pistol added to the already considerable ringing in my ears, and was itself followed by the flash and reflected heat of a beamer bolt.

Things quieted down after that. When the room had ceased to spin, I clambered carefully to my feet. Potnir, was down in one corner, his features contorted by pain, with a bullet hole in his right shoulder. The Dalgir was down too, but feeling no pain. He was dead, his upper torso burned away by a beamer. Ssaroth stood over him, the weapon in his hand. The sight of Ssaroth triggered a stray memory.

When the lights blazed on, the Dalgir had been looking directly at Hral Ssaroth. He had called out to our pseudo-Veck in shocked surprise.

He had called him by name!

CHAPTER 18

BAX moved to aid Potnir while Noor sat astride the fallen Baron. Ssaroth locked eyes with me and must have seen my thoughts there. His face contorted into a slow smile and he raised the beamer to point at my midsection.

"Help me here," Bax hissed from Potnir's side.

I gulped. "Bax . . . Noor, stand up *slowly*."

"What?" Bax twisted to look over his shoulder. He glanced at Ssaroth with the beamer, then at me, and confusion flashed across his face. Noor understood the situation immediately. He rose to his feet and backed away keeping his hands in sight.

"All of you against the wall," Ssaroth growled. He seemed to be enjoying himself as Bax and Noor hurried to comply. We were herded to one side of the room while Ssaroth backed to where he could watch us. Potnir lay in a pool of his own blood on the floor behind Ssaroth.

"What is happening here?" Bax demanded.

I took a deep breath for the first time in several seconds and tried to calm my heart. "I think that Hral Ssaroth is telling us he works for the other side. Am I right?"

Ssaroth laughed. "I had hoped to thwart your fishing expedition a bit more subtly. However, this will have to do now that I have been discovered."

Movement flickered at the edge of my vision.

"My first impression the day we met was right—you *are* a Dalgir, aren't you?"

"Obviously."

"What did you do with the real Ssaroth?"

"Real Ssaroth?"

"Of course! There never was a Taladoran agent named Hral Ssaroth, was there? The Dalgir lying dead at your feet knew you by name. But you were an imposter, 'Hral Ssaroth' would be the name of the Aasmoranian agent whose place you took. Therefore, the Time Watch computers must have been tampered with to insert your phony personnel file. Not difficult, I suppose, if the Empire has infiltrated the Watch."

My conjecture seemed plausible. After all, we were attempting to do essentially the same thing with our ferret. But why would any spy use his own name?

Ssaroth didn't give me a chance to ask the question. "You have no conception of how much effort has gone into creating this moment," he said as he raised the beamer to point directly at my face.

I lunged to one side and Ssaroth tumbled over backward, as Potnir flung himself into Ssaroth's legs. A beamer blast rent the air, then another.

When I regained my feet, Ssaroth was at the bottom of a pile of bodies and we had another corpse on our hands. Poor Potnir stared blindly upward, his chest smoking.

In a matter of seconds, Ssaroth was unconscious beside him and Bax was in possession of the devil's toy. He clutched it in one hand and gasped for breath.

The ferret picked that moment to signal job completion. I began disconnecting cables and putting things back the way they had been.

"Never mind that," Bax hissed. "Just pull out some of those wires so we can tie these two up before they regain consciousness."

I complied, feeling a bit foolish. We had captured the Baron and killed his guest of honor, so why try to be neat? Bax and Noor made surprisingly quick work of trussing our prisoners. The Baron was just coming around as they finished.

"What about Potnir?" Noor asked.

"Drag him back of those consoles over there," Bax said. "I'll tell Oraz how his son died—if any of us get out of here." He prodded the Baron with his boot. "Wake up, Excellency."

The Baron stirred. His eyes opened and he caught sight of the body beside him, and then Hral Ssaroth. For a moment he looked as if he would faint. "W-w-what is the meaning of this, Transtas?"

"I'll ask the questions, Excellency. Who was your friend, and what were you two doing here?"

"He is—was—Ambassador Ontoosa Mri of the Dalgiri Empire. The Ambassador had need to contact Brolis Base. Something about a stolen shuttle."

"Did you happen to mention our conversation of earlier this evening to the Ambassador?" Bax asked.

"Of course. Mri specifically requested that you be invited to his reception. When I confirmed that you had arrived, he insisted we come down here."

"And this other?" I asked.

Ylgost gulped. "I met him at Brolis Base with Mri three and a half years ago when the Dalgiri first came to this universe. He was Mri's commander."

"Don't you have that backward?" I asked. "Ssaroth must have worked for Mri."

"No. The Ambassador was this man's aide at that time."

"Cease your caterwauling, Ylgost!"

Bax turned to Ssaroth, who was glaring at the Governor. Someone had hung a mouse under one eye. I hoped it had been Potnir.

Bax turned to me. "What now?"

I scooped up the ferret. "We've got to get this to Dal Corst. Him also," I said, pointing to Ssaroth.

"It would be better to kill him."

"No! He must know how badly Taladoran security has been breached and why Dalgir is so interested in the Syllsin-Veck couplet. He's too valuable to kill—just yet, anyway." That last was for Ssaroth's benefit.

Bax stared at the prisoner and I began to fear I might have a mutiny on my hands. When he finally turned to Noor, it was with something approaching wistfulness in his expression. "Return to the reception and lead Felira and the woman emissary here. Do not attract attention."

Noor slipped out the door like a ghost and was gone.

"What now?" I asked Bax.

"We have to get you three out of here as quickly as we can. You take that one. . . ." He gestured at Ssaroth. "I will keep the other and use him to order the guards to lay down their weapons. After that we will try to extract our people before warships can be called in from Brolis and Veck."

Five minutes later there was a discreet tap on the door. Bax opened it while I covered him with the beamer. It was Noor with Jouniel and Felira.

We spent the next ten minutes embellishing Bax's plan. It was decided that Felira, Jouniel, and I would take Ssaroth and make our way to the roof. There, we would steal an aircar and light out for the farm where we had hidden our communicator.

Once at the farm, we would summon *City of Isvall* from her lair. In the meantime Bax and Noor would accompany the Governor back to the reception and force him to order the household troops to lay down their arms.

If all went well, about the time the Syllsintaag had taken Rossa-Home Stronghold, they would have a Taladoran fleet overhead to provide protection while the city was evacuated.

We sealed Ylgost's and Ssaroth's mouths with electrical tape I found in a tool cabinet and pushed them out the door. I led the way with the beamer, Jouniel and Ssaroth followed, and Felira brought up the rear. Jouniel had rigged a thin wire garrote around Ssaroth's neck so that all she had to do was give one sharp tug to choke him. The arrangement included a one-way slip knot. She had taken care to explain its operation and, for the moment, Ssaroth seemed happy to cooperate.

The corridors were still deserted, and we met no one until we reached the rooftop car park where two quick beamer bolts disposed of the guards. We dragged their bodies under the raised landing pad where they wouldn't be soon found, and stripped them of their weapons. Now the three of us were armed.

We hustled Ssaroth into a back seat of an aircar with Jouniel while Felira and I took the front.

"Can you fly one of these?" Felira asked.

"Hope so," I said. "Form follows function on most timelines, so this shouldn't be too different." I scanned the dot-dash Dalgiri script on the instrument panel, identifying controls and their functions. I was in luck. The car was functionally identical to a Taladoran model.

"Hold on, people, here we go," I yelled as I energized the lift-and-drives. The car rose sluggishly, as if the attitude drivers hadn't been properly calibrated, and headed off into the night.

I had forgotten that damned patrol flier! It was on us before we crossed the Rossa-Home city limits.

"Halt or be fired upon!" Was the command that issued from our speaker. At the same time, a light like a sun gone nova flashed on us. I took a deep breath and energized our comm unit.

"What dog dares challenge me?" I growled in my best Prussian officer style—my patented recipe for cowing underlings. Works every time.

Except this one.

"I repeat, stop or be fired upon!"

"This is the personal car of Ambassador Ontoosa Mri of the Dalgiri Empire. Fire on us and he will have you skinned."

"Please stop," the voice on the radio said, losing some of its composure. I let out a sigh and briefly congratulated myself on not being dead.

"Why?" I asked.

"You do not have clearance. I am required to stop all uncleared air vehicles."

"Come alongside," I said. "You can visually identify the Ambassador and then leave us to go about our business."

There was a long silence while the other pilot debated with himself. No streetwise American cop would have fallen for it, but then the Vecka were getting sloppy in their old age. Besides, we must have looked harmless.

The miniature sun astern changed position and began station-keeping off to our left. I ignored him for the time being as I frantically scanned the instrument panel.

"Where the hell did they hide the door jettisons, Jouniel?"

"Try under the dash, just above your right knee."

I found a lever and pulled hard. Several things happened at once. As the door separated, the slipstream nearly yanked me out of my seat and the car bucked wildly. The sudden yaw to the left probably saved our lives, for in the next instant the splat of hot lead punching through sheet metal overpowered the roar of the wind.

I fought my steed with one hand while aiming the beamer with the other. The window behind me exploded in a storm of broken glass as I squeezed the firing stud. I fired twice more and the searchlight went out as the patrol flier fell off on its side and headed in a steep dive for the ground.

I started to breathe again.

"Anybody hurt?"

"Just afterimages of the beamer bolt," Jouniel yelled from the backseat.

"No problem," Felira echoed from beside me.

"How's our guest?"

"We've got windscreen all over us back here, but he isn't seriously damaged, I'm sorry to say. That was good shooting, Duncan."

"We were lucky," I said, scanning the instruments once more. "Damn!"

"What's the matter?"

"We've been holed. If I'm reading this charge indicator right, I've got about two more minutes of flying time before we run out of juice."

I put the car down on her last ergs, skimming pseudoferns that would have made some of the lesser redwoods jealous. At the last second, a clearing intruded into the circle illuminated by the landing lights. I dropped the car into it and slid to a halt in a shower of weeds and grass.

By dawn we were ten miles from the wreck, and dead tired. We stopped to rest deep in the endless forest while Felira tried to figure out where we were.

"What do you think?" I asked.

"The farm is over that way," she said, pointing with the compass we had salvaged from the aircar. The distance was about fifty miles.

"Oh, my aching bunions."

"Shall we stop?" Jouniel asked.

"We have to stop," Felira said. "I can't walk another step."

I knew what she meant. My legs felt dead at the knees. The only comfort I took from our situation was that our prisoner looked worse than I did. "Okay, what say to four hours' rest and then we go on?"

There was no argument and everyone, Ssaroth included, slumped to the lichen-covered ground. I unslung the ferret from the makeshift pack I had built and used it for a pillow. After resting a bit, I ran over our options in my head.

We didn't have any.

Rossa-Home was closer than the farm, but we couldn't go there. An hour before dawn a flash lit the whole of the sky behind us. Minutes later the wind changed direction with a rush and the glow didn't die completely away for the better part of an hour. If Rossa-Home still existed, it was in enemy hands and chances were good that our friends were captives or dead.

We had nowhere to go but ahead. Fifty miles? Easy, really. A man in good condition can walk that in twenty hours on level ground. Only, this wasn't level ground. It would be four days before we reached the farm and summoned help from the fleet on the Moon. There was only one problem.

In four days the portal would be closed and the fleet gone.

I was startled out of my concentration by Hral Ssaroth's voice. Funny, but I had never noticed before how raspy it was. Which just goes to show that you'll overlook peculiarities in your friends, but not your enemies.

"Give up, MacElroy. You and the Taladoran woman will be treated as prisoners of war and given every consideration."

"And Felira?"

He laughed. "She's no concern of mine. If that fool Ylgost doesn't kill her, I might take her for my herd of slaves. I'm always on the lookout for good breeding stock."

I throttled the sudden anger that boiled within me, and forced myself to remain calm. "Watch your mouth. The only thing that stops me from carving that ugly face of yours with this beamer set on low is the fact that you are going to have to walk fifty miles under your own power."

"And if I refuse to walk?"

"I'll start carving now."

We locked eyes for a long minute. Finally, he blinked. "I'll walk."

Full dark at the end of the second day found us fifteen miles from our goal and ready to drop in our tracks.

Happiness is having a full belly and no blisters.

We had been following a wide slash in the endless fern forest, an area of low underbrush that meandered in the general direction we wanted to go. Felira had identified it as the scar of a wind-driven firestorm caused by a Veckan "object lesson." Just before dark we halted in a ruin that had once been a medium-size city.

A few wild berries grew among the crumbling walls and rusting steel. We gathered as many as we could find and split them four ways. Afterward, Jouniel and Felira went in search of a handy bush while I baby-sat the prisoner.

"Are you asleep?" Ssaroth asked, his words slurred by a puffy lower lip where a low-lying branch had caught him earlier in the day.

"Don't you wish?" I asked, glancing toward him.

"An interesting place, this, is it not?"

"I suppose." In truth, I was so tired I wouldn't have been interested in a proposition by the reigning Hollywood sex bomb.

"Look around you, MacElroy. Here dwelt enemies of Dalgir."

"You mean enemies of Veck, don't you?"

"They were once Dalgiri and will be again, sooner than they realize."

"So much for 'honor among thieves,' " I said, not really surprised. Cozying up to the Empire was like going to bed with a boa constrictor—you generally woke up in the middle of a squeeze play. "What about this place?"

"It would be a shame if this ruin were San Francisco, or Los Angeles, or Detroit."

I lifted my droopy eyelids and peered through the gathering gloom. "I don't remember telling you about my home."

"You didn't."

"Then you must have gone to a lot of trouble to find out those names. Why?"

"If only you knew how much trouble . . . Perhaps someday I will tell you."

"This wouldn't happen to be the preamble to a recruiting speech, would it?"

"Why not?"

"If we are going to be on the same side, perhaps you will explain what is going on."

"Come now, you don't really expect me to expend all my bargaining counters while still a prisoner, do you? Help me against the Taladoran, and I will consider us allies."

"Then I guess the deal's off. You have no reason to trust me, and I have every reason to distrust you. You tried to kill me, remember? Hardly a good basis for a partnership is it?"

Ssaroth started to say something else, then shut up as we heard Felira and Jouniel making their way back. Jouniel double-checked his bonds before easing down beside me.

"Did you two have a nice chat while we were gone?"

"Sure," I said. "Ssaroth offered me a job."

"You didn't take it, I hope."

"Couldn't. Have to give up too much self-respect."

I took the first watch while the others tried to get some sleep. It was one of those evenings that drive poets to rhapsody, when the stars seem endless and Venus hangs like a twenty-carat diamond above the western horizon. The Moon was in its first quarter and I passed the time trying to pick out the places where the fleet was hidden. I soon tired of that, made myself as comfortable as you can get while sitting on a pile of bricks, leaned back, and stargazed.

I don't know how long it was before I realized that Orion the Hunter had an extra star in his right foot. I felt a mild exhilaration at the thought that I was seeing a newborn nova. I nursed my excitement as long as I could—to combat sleep—but the feeling wore off and I resumed my search of the heavens.

Within fifteen minutes I had identified at least six other

stars I didn't remember. So much for my nova hypothesis. Something was very, very wrong with this universe. Either that, or . . .

"MacElroy," I muttered to myself, "your mind has finally snapped."

Somehow I managed to keep my eyes open until midnight, when I shook Jouniel awake to stand the next watch.

She roused fitfully. "Anything to report?"

"Just that the stars are out of position," I mumbled as I lay down next to Felira.

I seem to remember vaguely that Jouniel answered "Yes, I know," but it could have been my imagination. I was asleep before my head reached the ferret, which I was still using as a pillow.

CHAPTER 19

"WAKE up, Duncan!"

I roused to the sound of Felira's voice and opened my eyes to darkness lit only by starlight.

"What's up?" I whispered.

"I think I saw a Veckan shuttle."

That brought me wide awake in a hurry. "When?"

"Just now. There were three bright flashes over the horizon. I glanced up and there it was."

"Where and how fast?"

"Just above the tops of the trees in the direction of Rossa-Home. I think it was hovering. At least, it didn't get any bigger while I could still see it. What do we do now?"

"We get the hell out of here!"

I shook Jouniel awake and then our prisoner, explaining the situation in as few words as possible. I made it clear to Ssaroth that I would brook no trouble from him. Then we moved out, striding as quickly as we could in the darkness. Unfortunately, that turned out to be little better than a slow creep.

I called a halt as soon as the eastern sky had lightened sufficiently to make out the distant mountains around us. There was nothing in sight except a few big pseudopterodactyls. We rested just long enough to catch our breath and gather a few gulps of berries before pushing on.

Within a mile the fire slash petered out and we reentered thick forest. We had traveled about five miles when Felira, who had taken over the lead, silently signaled a halt.

"What is it?" Jouniel whispered.

"I think I saw something," Felira whispered back.

"Go to cover," I commanded, diving into the undergrowth by the side of the animal trail we had been following.

We lay for ten minutes, anxiously searching for signs of movement ahead. Nothing. I was about to order the trek continued when Jouniel gasped in a sharp intake of breath.

"What?"

"I'm not sure. Could have been an animal."

"It was no animal," Felira said, her voice barely audible from five feet away. "I can see a man in a green uniform. I don't recognize the livery. Could be a serf from a household I don't know, maybe Aylthern Continent."

I craned my neck to look, but could see nothing through the dense foliage. I unpocketed my beamer as the women did likewise with their captured slug-throwers. We held a hurried eye-conference with each other. That was a mistake.

In the excitement we had forgotten Ssaroth.

I've got to give him his due. If he suffered from personality defects, indecisiveness wasn't one of them. Sensing that his chances of escape were as good as they would ever get, he seized the leash with his teeth and pulled it from Jouniel's grasp. Suddenly he was up and sprinting forward, dodging awkwardly with hands still tied behind his back.

"Halt!" I screamed, reverting to English in my exitement. Ssaroth was already two trees away, and dodging for cover. I snapped up my beamer almost without thinking.

"No!" Jouniel hissed. "We need him alive."

"But he's getting away!"

"Can't be helped," she said. "We came to discover how much Dalgir has learned from Veck. Ssaroth is the key to that mystery and many others."

"He doesn't do us any good now that he's escaped."

"Nor would he if he were dead, Duncan. Let us worry about ourselves and find someplace to make a stand."

"Where?"

"There's a defensible position half a mile back," Felira said.

We ran that half-mile, heedless of the whipping branches or entangling roots across the trail. We didn't stop until we had belly flopped into a depression in the flat forest floor just big enough for the three of us. I gasped for breath at the same time I checked the beamer's charge indicator.

"Ammunition check," I called out. "Felira?"

"Nine rounds."

"Jouniel?"

"Seven."

"And I've got seven, too. That's twenty-three. Let's make them count."

"Jouniel and I will empty our weapons," Felira said. "You be sure to save three of those charges, Duncan."

I opened my mouth to ask why, then shut it. I knew what Felira had in mind—namely that a beamer is surer than a bullet in the mouth. I had always disparaged Hollywood horse operas for being overly melodramatic when, during the Indian attack, the hero runs out of ammunition save for a single cartridge each for himself and the heroine. But now that I found myself in a similar situation, it seemed the only logical thing to do.

Considering that Veck routinely reduced rebellious towns to their component atoms, what would they do to us for killing the Dalgiri Ambassador and kidnaping Hral Ssaroth?

We lay in silence for a long time before I reached out and took Felira by the hand.

"I'm sorry," I said.

"For what?" she asked.

"For the way things have turned out."

She considered that for a few seconds, and then half smiled. "I would rather live, Duncan. But if that is not to be, I am glad that I will be dying with friends."

I leaned over to kiss her. We were interrupted by Jouniel's hiss.

"Shush, I see something."

"How many?" I asked, my gaze following Jouniel's.

"Can't tell. All I catch sight of is an occasional rustling of bushes. Whoever they are, they're good."

"Duncan."

"Yes?" I asked, turning my gaze back to Felira.

"I love you."

"I love you, too."

"Get ready," Jouniel said, tensing. "I think they've spotted us. Here they come. . . ."

I felt the world whirl around me as a full dozen green-suited figures materialized out of the brush and walked steadily toward us. It was all I could do to stand to greet them.

They were Taladoran Marines.

The noncom leading the patrol walked warily toward us, regarding me as if I were some kind of tiger ready to pounce. "You Duncan MacElroy?"

"That's me," I said. I did my best to keep from grinning like an idiot, but I don't think I succeeded. Truth is, I could have kissed them all, I was so happy to see them.

"Academician Soufilcar Jouniel?" the marine asked next, his eyes flicking between Jouniel and Felira, his tone doubtful. It took a second before I realized what was bothering him. Jouniel's disguise had proved remarkably resistant to the rigors of our trek. I appeared to be in the company of two Syllsintaag ladies.

"Here, Centurion," Jouniel said. "What are you doing here? The fleet was to stay on the Moon until I called."

The centurion shrugged. "Those who command do not explain their motives to lowly mudfeet such as myself, Academician. Scuttlebutt has it that we intercepted a message for help from the local cragfaces to their litter mates on the next timeline over. Commander Corst ordered us down to engage their fleet as soon as it appeared on our detectors. That was two days ago.

"*Jerrap*, what a fight! We pounced on 'em like a hunting *tork* back home. Blew 'em to plasma."

"Any casualties on our side?"

"We lost a few aboard *Kreshni* to a near-miss. *City of Ool* sprung some hull plates, too. Nothing serious enough to stop us from heading for home come nightfall, though. I'll feel better when we get back to civilization."

"Do you know about the natives, Centurion?" Felira asked. "Were many killed?"

"You must be Lady Felira Transtas."

"Yes. Do you have word of my father?"

"Commander Corst sent a message with all the search parties, my lady. Your father is safe and the evacuation of Rossa-Home has begun. Casualties at the stronghold were light."

"What about Ssaroth?"

"Who?"

"The Dalgir who was with us. Did you get him?"

The marine grinned and nodded. "He practically stumbled into our arms. Seemed a bit indignant about the whole thing until one of my men tapped him on the head."

"Where is he now, Centurion?" Jouniel asked.

"Under guard in a clearing a ways back. I've got a shuttle putting down there in a few bora. We'd best hurry."

The shuttle was a hundred-passenger troop transport. Most of the marines curled up in their couches and went to sleep the instant we boarded. Jouniel excused herself and went forward to talk to the flagship on the communicator. The unconscious Ssaroth was laid out under guard in a rear compartment. That left me alone with Felira in a little island of empty seats next to one of the few windows in the boxy craft. We leaned forward, pressing our noses against the plastic as the miles we had crossed so laboriously floated by in an effortless procession below.

She turned to look at me as I slipped my arm around her waist. Our faces were just six inches apart. "We've got a decision to make—and quickly," I whispered.

"Decision?"

"Don't be coy, Felira. We haven't the time. I want a straight answer. Will you be leaving with the fleet when it lifts off for Talador tonight?"

She hesitated for a long time, searching my face with her eyes. I knew the answer even before she spoke. Maybe I had known it all along and refused to admit it.

"I'm sorry, Duncan. *I can't.*"

"Why not?"

"I would be deserting my people. How could I look at myself in a mirror after what I've done to them."

"What have you done?" I asked.

"I am responsible for bringing your fleet here and talking Father into supporting you. It is my doing that we Syllsintaag now suffer the wrath of Veck."

"You are not responsible—Dal, Jouniel, and I are."

She looked at me, her eyes glistening brightly from the tears that welled up in them. "It would have been better if I had died on the Moon, Duncan."

"Dammit, Felira, I love you and I won't have you talking foolishness!"

I didn't realize I had been yelling until I noticed several grizzled faces pivot in our direction. I clenched my teeth and shut up. Felira sobbed quietly, her face buried in my shoulder, as Rossa-Home appeared over the horizon. In less than ten minutes, we had traveled the same distance that had taken us three agonizing days on foot.

City of Isvall was hovering over the city like a great steel basketball. Small dark shapes moved back and forth between the flagship and the ground. Other shuttles and landing craft could be seen on the ground with long lines of people making ready to board.

After the previous three weeks, the familiar austerity of *Isvall*'s companionways seemed claustrophobic as we made our way toward the center of the great sphere and the main control room.

Dal Corst pushed himself back from the captain's console as we were ushered into the nerve center of the dreadnought.

"So my wayward team has finally decided to come home? For a while there I thought I had lost you."

"You and me both," I said, grinning as I returned his pummeling.

"Follow me and we will get you three debriefed," he said, turning to leave by a different hatchway. We moved to a cramped conference room a few feet down the passageway, arraying ourselves around a briefing table.

"Where is the ferret?" Dal asked.

"The marines escorted us to the computer lab on the way here," Jouniel said. "We handed it over to the chief correlationist."

"Begin your report then, Team Leader."

Jouniel reported everything that had transpired from

the moment we'd left the farm until the raiding party left the great hall. At that point, she turned the narrative over to me. When I had finished Dal's face fell into a deep scowl.

"This Baron Ylgost said Ssaroth had commanded the Dalgiri expedition to Syllsin-Veck? Any chance of his being mistaken?"

"You didn't have to look down the barrel of that beamer," I said. "No mistake."

Dal turned to his intercom. "Irtok."

The speaker came alive instantly. "Here, Dal."

"Have you got the ferret's information copied yet?"

"Copied and distributed to every ship in the fleet per your orders."

"Then prepare a literature search for any mention of the original Dalgiri expedition to the Syllsin-Veck couplet with special attention to the senior officers. Give that search a Priority One and then run the one we talked about earlier."

"The search for records of the recent combined Dalgiri-Veckan military operation?"

"Right. Codename Civilization X—any report on the location, capabilities, or inhabitants thereof. Use any member of the battle staff you need. I want answers yesterday."

"Acknowledged and understood."

Dal turned to me as the intercom went dead. "Where is Ssaroth now?"

"Nursing a headache aboard the transport."

Dal pressed the intercom control again.

"Security!"

"At your service, Commander."

"Have you been notified about the traitor Ssaroth?"

"Acknowledged."

"I want him probed by your most skilled technician."

The security duty officer's face was replaced on the screen by that of Qoth Eyb, *Isvall*'s chief of security.

"You understand the danger of that, Dal? If he is truly a Dalgiri agent, he will have been conditioned against psychprobing. He could be permanently damaged."

"I need information that can only be had from him

and I need it before we lift for home! Get it any way you can."

"Understood."

Dal turned to us. "Anyone think of anything I've forgotten?"

We all gestured our various negatives.

"What is the tactical situation?" Jouniel asked.

"Stable for the moment," he said. "After we defeated the fleet sent to rescue Rossa-Home Stronghold from Bax Transtas, I sent *City of Ool* and *Zirca* to guard the portal from Veck. That will keep the enemy's home fleet bottled up until we abandon this timeline. Luckily, that secondary portal here on the surface of Syllsin—the one they used to go after Civilization X—is closed at the moment. The Lunar portal is open, of course, but we know where that leads and they can't strike at us through it. I'm delaying our departure until just before the Lunar portal closes in order to cover the Syllsintaag evacuation."

The intercom sounded and Dal turned to it. "Grafftar Transtas sends his compliments and reports the evacuation is going more slowly than expected. He asks if we can spare a few more boats to transport his people to the dispersal points?"

"Give him what you can." Dal turned to Felira. "Do you want to speak to your father?"

"Yes, and join him as soon as possible."

"I'll have you guided back to the landing bays where a scout is waiting to take you down."

Felira got up to leave.

"Wait a minute," I said, rising also. "I'll take you."

"Let someone else do that," Dal said, his manner gruff. "I need you here."

I shook my head. "You don't understand. I'm not helping her to the scout. I'm going all the way to the surface with her."

"When will you be back?" Dal's expression reflected his suspicion.

"I won't. I'm staying on Syllsin . . . permanently."

CHAPTER 20

DAL looked like a restaurant patron who has just bitten into a rancid steak but is too polite to spit it out in public. His gaze flicked quickly from me to Felira and back again.

"So that's how it is?"

I nodded.

"I should have known. Jouniel warned me that first day you returned to Jafta that Felira's attraction to you might prove contagious. Have you considered your destiny in making this decision?"

I shook my head. "It was always your idea that I have a destiny, Dal. Never mine."

He considered that for a moment before answering. "That first night we met, I explained why I think you are a marked man. Nothing has happened to change my opinion."

Felira listened to our increasingly heated exchange with growing confusion.

"Would someone please tell me what is going on here?"

Dal gestured toward her with his eyes. "Tell her."

So I did. Even as I told it, the whole thing had an aura of unreality about it; as if it were the script for one of those Japanese monster movies they play on the Saturday morning kiddie shows.

How's this for a plot, L.B.? The hero's an ordinary Joe—no Einstein, yuh understand—who goes out for a beer and never comes back. Instead he meets this beautiful spy from the future, or Mars, or Alpha Centauri, wherever the hell that is, and he saves her from the villains. The villains are real ugly bastards, you see, and afterwards the broad rewards this shnook by telling him he's really a handsome prince in disguise, and they go off together to her magic kingdom beyond the stars. I tell you it's dynamite, L.B., and all I need to get the production rolling is a measly million and a half! . .

I finished up with: "Dal thinks that because the goon squad's mission was to cash in my life insurance, somehow that proves I'm going to live to be a hundred and three and win the war for the Confederation."

"The fact that the 'goon squad' as you call them was from the future validates such an opinion," Dal said when I had finished. "Using retrograde universes was no stroke of genius on the part of the Near Men. What keeps us from being inundated by hordes of our descendants is the fact that retrograde universes are one-way streets. There is no going back.

"Can you blame us then for becoming interested when we learned that our hereditary enemies had gone to such great lengths to kill one insignificant outtimer? Or later, when that outtimer began to display a penchant for being in the right place at the right time?—If you consider it objectively, Duncan, you are probably the luckiest human being alive."

I laughed. "Lucky? Me? Accident-prone is more like it. I've had two aircars shot from under me in the last four years; and you know damned well what happened on the Fyalsorn expedition. You were there!"

Dal nodded. "I bear the scars. I also know that you have not been seriously injured in any of your misadventures. We've spoken before of the likelihood of your being with Jana Dougwaix when the Dalgiri assassins found you. But the clincher is the monumental violation of the laws of chance that occurred when you rescued Felira from certain death on the Moon. You couldn't come to the aid of just any damsel in distress. You had to stumble across the one—the *only one,* mind you—who could lead us directly to the timeline that had invented the teleportation generator, the one place we most wanted to go!"

Dal paused to catch his breath. I opened my mouth to say something, and then closed it again. Dammit, if he wasn't right! I should have been killed a dozen times over since the night Jana and I had disposed of the body of a dead man with sloping eye ridges and a glass-barreled pistol. No wonder I was beginning to think of my life as something from an old and not very good movie.

Dal shook his head in apparent sadness, and stared with compassion at Felira.

"I'm afraid that Duncan's destiny lies with Talador. When this vessel leaves Syllsin to return home, he will be aboard. He has no choice in the matter. I am sorry for you both, but the Fates are not always kind to those they have taken for their own."

The tension in the briefing room had risen until it was almost palpable. Sensing that positions were hardening until there would be no backing down, Dal abruptly changed his tack. One instant he was red in the face, his temper barely under control; the next he was cool and all cheek-to-cheek smile.

"Look, even if I'm wrong, the least you two can do is stay until the day is over. How about it, Felira? I need Duncan's help in unraveling this Hral Ssaroth disaster. Surely you can wait until nightfall to see your father."

Dal didn't fool either of us. He was playing for time, betting I would change my mind or, barring that, that Felira would. I could see Felira hesitate, and I myself was about to tell him what he could do with his offer, when she agreed to his request. Calm settled over the briefing room after that, lasting through lunch. Qoth Eyb showed up during the meal with a sour look on his face.

"What's happened?" Dal asked the moment he saw Eyb's expression.

"Ssaroth *was* conditioned against hypnoprobe. I'm afraid we didn't get much out of him, Dal."

"Is he dead?"

"No, but he has lapsed into catatonia."

"Permanent?"

"Don't know. Maybe, given sufficient time, we could rouse him. . . ."

"Never mind, Qoth. Did you get anything before he went under?"

"Nothing much that makes sense. Nightmare stuff mostly, and the impression that the Syllsin-Veck couplet is very important to him. We were exploring *that* when we hit the conditioning block and lost him. I blame myself for it. The block is of a type I've never seen before, and I thought I knew everything about how a human mind can be booby-trapped."

"What about the ferret? Get anything from that?"

Qoth had been uncomfortable while talking about Ssaroth. He shifted his weight several times and refused to meet Dal's gaze. Obviously, he wasn't used to reporting failure and didn't care for the experience. At the mention of our purloined Veckan computer-net data, he perked up.

"Quite a lot, actually. According to the Veckan historical records, their ancestors were a large military colony sent at the direct command of the Emperor himself. If the purpose is recorded, we haven't found it yet."

"Sent here? How? What series of universes gave them access to Syllsin-Veck three centuries ago, and why haven't we heard of this expedition before?"

"Not 'series of universes,' Dal—universe, singular." Qoth reeled off a long timeline coordinate. Dal's face suddenly developed a vacant look.

"Where have I heard that number before?" he asked.

"Perhaps in one of the technical journals. The place has a nasty climate due to an advanced state of glaciation. It's a high-rate retrograde—"

Dal's open palm slammed to the table top. "Of course! That was the timeline we investigated in Duncan's case."

Dal turned to me. "After Jana reported what she had learned, the Council ordered a complete investigation."

I nodded. "Tasloss told me as much the day I was summoned to his office."

"Did he tell you that part of that investigation was an attempt to identify the retrograde timeline that the assassins used to work their little miracle? We never did—not enough data. But we had a favored candidate. It appears that it was the same timeline that the Dalgiri used as a vehicle to colonize Veck three hundred years ago." Dal stopped and my world wobbled around me as I realized the punch line.

"Don't you see? *The Vecka are from the same future as the Dalgiri who tried to kill you!*"

I gulped. No wonder Talador had never heard of them! Of course they spoke a language more modern than today; flew aircars that looked like next year's model; built computers more advanced than they had any right to! "Wouldn't it take decades to ride a retrograde that far into the past?"

"Longer, Duncan," Qoth said. "More than a century on that particular timeline. How much more would depend on how far in the future they came from. Obviously, they used cold-sleep techniques."

"The Dalgiri spent a century in cold sleep just to kill me?"

"No, of course not," Dal said. "The century was needed to *enter* the Veckan timeline three hundred years ago. Twenty years on the retrograde would have sufficed to reach Europo-American."

Dal glanced at Jouniel. She was an island of calm in a sea of confusion. "You aren't surprised to discover the Vecka are from our future, are you, Jouniel?" Dal asked.

"Not true. I am flabbergasted. However, it does fit rather nicely with a theory of mine."

"Which is?"

"That the Syllsin-Veck couplet itself is the reason for everything that has happened lately, of course. Look at the evidence. Our hypnoprobe of Ssaroth revealed only that Syllsin-Veck is special to him for some reason. The future Dalgiri will go to heroic efforts to colonize it centuries before their time. And what of Duncan's attackers? They too were future Dalgiri. Could it be they were trying to kill him to prevent his rescuing Felira and thus leading Taladorans to this universe?

"Then there are Syllsin's rather peculiar fauna and flora. Only one explanation would seem to account for all the things wrong with this timeline. . . ." She looked at each of us in turn, pausing for dramatic effect. "It seems to me that we may soon find ourselves with adversaries more powerful than even the Dalgiri. And there is a good chance they won't be human!"

The only sound in the briefing room was the quiet hum of *Isvall* herself.

"Would you care to explain that?" Dal asked in a deceptively mild voice.

Jouniel nodded. "Look around you. This timeline is absolutely unique. Its life forms are unlike any we have encountered before. So are those on Veck, according to the Syllsintaag. Whatever the mechanism that has populated all other timelines with similar kinds of life, it obviously doesn't work here. Why not?

"Simple, really. The timelines in a cluster core have very stable portals. Cross-pollination goes on all the time and local evolutionary differences tend to damp out quickly. Skewlines like Syllsin-Veck, however, wander in and out of contact with many different universes, infecting (and being infected by) each in turn.

"This line has been fertilized by a vast number of universes over the last billion years. The variation is so great, in fact, that the evidence points to our having discovered a whole new order of Paratime structure. Up to now, we've recognized single timelines, timeline couplets, interdependent clusters of a few dozen to several thousand universes. Yet all the universes of Paratime so far discovered are closely related. It's as if all known universes are members of some local association, some closely bound grouping of timelines whose structure is too big for us to see clearly.

"But if this grouping doesn't extend infinitely across Paratime, then there must be other such groupings, macroclusters of timelines unrelated to our own. If such a situation exists, then the timelines on the edges of such macroclusters should be seeded with life from both sides of the boundary. I think Syllsin is just such a universe."

Dal was skeptical. "The discovery of a few new species isn't much on which to build a whole next higher order of Paratime structure, Jouniel."

Jouniel laughed. "The oddities in the local flora and fauna just got me thinking about the whole subject. Duncan, tell Dal what you discovered last night while on guard duty."

"Huh?" I asked.

"The stars."

"Oh, the stars! They aren't where they are supposed to be."

Dal looked as if I had stabbed him.

Jouniel smiled. "When was the last time we discovered a timeline where the heavens were out of place?"

"Never."

"Yet logic says the pattern of everything should be random from universe to universe, does it not? Why should the sun, the stars, even the farthest galaxies always be in the same position in every universe?"

"I've never thought about it."

"None of us has. Yet it's a puzzle every bit as perplexing as the replication of life forms. Probably it's an effect of the local distribution of matter and energy in our own neighborhood of 5-space. But if so, the effect is purely local. Isn't it therefore logical to assume that any universe from beyond our local neighborhood could have different constellations in its sky?"

"*And Syllsin does!*" I said.

"And then there is the evidence of the Syllsintaag themselves. What archeology they have done dates the earliest traces of humanity to about fifty thousand years ago."

Dal considered it for a moment. "Then this Civilization X that the Dalgiri attacked—it must be in the next macrocluster over!"

"A good tentative hypothesis," Jouniel agreed. "And the Empire is interested in *this* universe because it's the gateway to that other cluster."

Dal groaned. "Then that makes Syllsin just as important to us. If there is a civilization more powerful than our own out there, we will need to know everything we can about it."

Jouniel nodded. "Only, when we send in our scouts, we'd better caution them about what to expect.

"Let's never forget that *Homo sapiens* may be a strictly local phenomenon, too!"

CHAPTER 21

From: Commander, Syllsin expedition.
To: The Ruling Council.
Message begins: Have decided to defend this time-
line against heavy force of Veckan and possibly
Dalgiri warships. Imperative that a rescue expedition
be dispatched as soon as a secure series of transitions
from Talador to Syllsin can be surveyed. Will dis-
patch courier shuttle with information so far obtained
and full report. Message ends.
                    Signed: Dal Corst, Commanding

If anyone ever writes a definitive history of the brief
and brutal Syllsin-Veck war, they will probably split it
in two because that was essentially the way we fought it:
the Taladoran fleet had more than it could handle defend-
ing the portal from Veck, so the Syllsintaag were pretty
much on their own to mop up the surprisingly strong resistance put together by the surviving Veckan governors.

The two campaigns couldn't have been more different.

Fleet action began within hours of Dal's decision to
stay. The whole of the Veckan Navy seemed to be lined
up on the other side of the portal, each ship eager to get
its crack at us. Luckily for us, the nature of temporal portals is such that no matter how big the enemy fleet, it still
had to come through in single file—just like a row of
ducks in a shooting gallery.

Not that we got away without cost to our side. One of
the hundred or so vessels destroyed in the first week's
fighting was the Taladoran cruiser *Kreshni,* the victim of a

lucky shot—a Golden BB in the parlance of my home-land.

After the possibility that we would be swept aside by an overwhelming force at the primary portal, our biggest worry—and the cause of many sleepless nights—was what to do when the portal to Civilization X reopened in the spring.

Somewhere beyond that portal was an immensely powerful civilization, possibly alien, almost surely mad as hell at the Dalgiri. If they had traced the Dalgiri back to Syllsin, we could easily find ourselves hip deep in aliens intent on exterminating any human they could get their tentacles on.

So on the morning the temporal energy flow shifted between universes and the Syllsin–Civilization X portal reopened for business, our small fleet was poised for battle. Apparently the superbeings beyond the gate were either still preparing, or not as angry as we thought. To our great relief, our preparations were in vain.

It wasn't long afterward that the Veckan fleet calculated its losses and decided it had had enough.

The Veckan ground forces soon did likewise, having been beaten in a series of pitched battles with Bax Transtas's Army of Free Syllsin. Eventually they found themselves, backs to the sea, in a barren corner of the Aylthern Continent. They surrendered—with much spirited haggling over terms—but only after finding the imposing silhouette of *City of Ool* over their positions, ready to rain fire down around their heads.

Two weeks later the Syllsin Lunar portal reopened and a hundred Taladoran ships poured through to relieve our beleaguered fleet.

CHAPTER 22

THE soft night breeze wafted gently across the roof-top garden, bringing with it the scent of roses, jasmine, and the pungent aroma of a small white flower that has no duplicate in any other known universe. Felira and I sat amid the greenery and looked out across the glittering lights of Transtas Keep as a gibbous moon climbed the eastern sky.

Along with the scent of flowers, the wind carried the sound of revelry from the town square two blocks away. All Transtas Keep had gathered there in a riotous crowd intent on celebrating the birth of Free Syllsin. Their hero, Bax Transtas, had just returned from the Aylthern Continent that morning and the party showed signs of running all night.

Felira and I were holding our own reunion in the roof-top garden. She had acted as aide-de-camp to her father during the hostilities, and Dal Corst had kept me busy with the Taladoran fleet, with the result that we hadn't seen each other in six months.

It had been the longest six months of my life.

"Did you miss me?" I asked when we were finally alone after the day's interminable public ceremonies.

"More than anything," Felira sighed huskily as she snuggled close. She was still attired in the camouflage greens of the Army of Free Syllsin, the equivalent of captain's bars on her collar. I wore the unadorned gray of the Time Watch.

"Dal took me to see Hral Ssaroth yesterday."

"How is he, Duncan?"

"Better, but still a basket case as far as I'm concerned.

He is talking now, but rambles on aimlessly for hours. He still doesn't respond to direct questions."

"It would have been kinder to kill him."

"Remember the 'nightmare images' Qoth spoke of that last day together aboard *Isvall?* They are getting worse. The medtechs are worried that one of these times he won't pull out of a seizure. Dal's beginning to wonder if the image is a figment of Ssaroth's imagination, or something he's really seen."

"Something he's seen?"

"Perhaps an inhabitant of Civilization X. If so, on that timeline intelligence must have descended from something mightily like a *Tyrannosaurus rex,* to judge from the fragmentary descriptions they've been getting. Dal wants to take Ssaroth back to Jafta next month when *City of Isvall* leaves. They have the facilities to really wring him out there." I hesitated an instant before broaching the next subject.

"Dal's asked me to go along, too."

"Will you?"

"That depends on the next few minutes."

"I don't understand."

I took her hands into mine. "I'm asking you to marry me. Whether I go or not depends on your answer."

Felira's reaction wasn't quite what I had expected. She hesitated for the span of two heartbeats as she searched my eyes with her own. It was almost as if she was waiting for the punch line to a particularly malicious joke.

"What of your destiny?"

"You know Jouniel's theory. She thinks the Dalgiri were after me because I would one day rescue you, that maybe I looked like the weakest link in the chain of events that led to Free Syllsin. If true, my 'destiny' went up in smoke the instant I laid eyes on you. From that moment on, I was just another poor innocent victim of circumstance, like everybody else."

Felira searched my eyes for a few seconds more. Then I found myself smothered in wet kisses and warm woman.

"Does this mean you will?" I asked when I could breathe again.

"What do you think?"

We sealed the bargain with another kiss—with several

in fact. Finally, when the world had ceased to spin around us and I had begun to notice my surroundings once more, Felira broke the embrace.

"We should immediately ask Father for his blessing as Lawgiver of Transtas Sept, so the banns may be posted. I'm sure he will give us dispensation from the normal waiting period in order to have the ceremony before *Isvall* leaves."

I smiled. "You go ahead. I'll be down shortly. I have some things to do before I greet my future father-in-law."

She kissed me again, this time lightly on the cheek. "Hurry as soon as you can. We don't want to be late for the Ceremony of Homecoming."

With that, she was gone and I was left alone to gaze out over the city and think. I needed time to put my emotions in order before joining the celebration. The problem was that I hadn't been entirely truthful with Felira about what I had learned during my visit to Ssaroth's cell.

Ssaroth was huddled next to his bunk, shivering in fright, when the marines admitted Dal and me. Enemy or no, I couldn't help feeling sorry for that poor, quavering mass of protoplasm that had once been a man. Felira was right. He would have been better off dead.

"Can't something be done for him, Dal?"

"No."

It must have been the sound of my voice, or Dal's, or maybe Ssaroth was just due for one of his bouts of near-sanity. Whatever it was, something sparked his attention. He looked up and saw us standing there, and his eyes lost their empty look for just a second.

"Rimbrick, is that you?"

The name was like a cannon shot going off inside my skull. *RIMBRICK!* That was the Dalgir I had killed in the toolshed back of my uncle's cabin.

Then the moment was gone and Ssaroth slumped back into semi-coma again. Dal gestured toward the door and I followed him out.

"Is that why you brought me here today?" I demanded as Dal led me through *Isvall*'s bustling corridors. He refused to answer me until we had returned to his shipboard office.

"Yes, that was why I summoned you, Duncan. I thought you would like to know. We always wondered whether there were more than four Dalgiri after you that night. The mystery is no more. The assassination squad numbered five and one of them was Hral Ssaroth."

I had thought I was immune to emotional shock by then. I was wrong. Suddenly my knees were rubber and I thumped down hard in the chair in front of Dal's desk.

"How did you get it out of him?"

"We didn't. He started rambling on about the Europo-American mission three days ago, and our facts are far from complete. Still, we have pieced together quite a lot of the story as details floated up out of his fractured subconscious. Everything that has happened to you for the last four and a half years has been related—Ssaroth, Rimbrick, the rest of the Death Squad, and the Veckan military colony. All of these originated within the future Dalgiri Empire at approximately the same time, for reasons we do not as yet understand.

"Ssaroth was in command of the Death Squad. He used the expedition's shuttle as his command post while his minions staked out places where you were likely to be. You know what happened that night better than anyone. Then after you had escaped the trap and made your way to the Confederation, Ssaroth somehow managed to flee to Dalgir. His purpose appears to have been to guide the Dalgiri to Veck three hundred years after it was colonized.

"After he hammered out the alliance that led to the Dalgiri-Veckan raid on Civilization X, he obtained the help of the Dalgiri Navy to complete his primary mission —killing you.

"You were then at the Academy. Since he couldn't reach you any other way, Ssaroth had the Fyalsorn research base established and launched the shuttle with the newly obtained teleportation generator in a raid against the Academy. Something went wrong and the raider blundered into our fixed batteries at the Salfa Prime portal before he realized where he was. It could have been a sensor failure, or just a mixup in orders. Whichever, instead of destroying the Academy and you along with it, the raid merely acted as the catalyst that led to Talador's gaining possession of the teleportation generator."

I whistled softly, off-key. "Persistent bastard, wasn't he?"

Dal nodded. "After the Fyalsorn disaster, he decided that your death required his personal attention. He enlisted the Dalgiri intelligence service in a scheme to smuggle him into Watch Headquarters. It's ironic. *I* tried to break you loose from the engineers for two years without success. Apparently, the orders detaching you from lunar-fortification duty were initiated by Ssaroth's henchman in the records section."

I shook my head. "I don't get it. Ssaroth had plenty of opportunity to kill me. Why didn't he? For that matter, after Felira showed us where Syllsin is, why would he care anymore? The damage was done."

"You're wrong."

"But Jouniel said—"

"Jouniel is wrong. As for why he didn't kill you before we left Jafta or on any of several opportunities before the night of Baron Ylgost's reception, I can only surmise that he was having second thoughts. After all, your record of narrow escapes would give any assassin pause. Besides, in spite of his mission, Ssaroth appears to have liked you."

"Huh? He picked a funny way to show it."

"It's the truth. We are monitoring his emotional responses during his ramblings. Each day brings additional memories to the surface and provides us with more data. A shadowy figure is beginning to emerge from Ssaroth's ravings; a mover and shaker; a George Washington or Abraham Lincoln or Winston Churchill.

"That figure is *you*, Duncan."

"But *why?*"

"We don't know. Ssaroth's ramblings generally lack the referents that would enable us to understand them. About the only thing that comes through clearly is that you seem to be the central player in this drama."

My discussion with Dal had taken place twenty-four hours earlier, and I was still shivering at Dal's words. Truth is, I didn't *feel* like a mover and shaker. But then again, what does greatness feel like? Did Napoleon or

George Washington or Albert Einstein really feel any different inside than "normal" people do? And what if my role model was to be more on the order of Genghis Khan or Attila the Hun or Adolf Hitler?

Even the possibility scared me spitless. But the human mind is a wondrous machine. Given enough time, a person can convince himself of anything. After a while the fit of blue funk wore off a bit and I began to feel better about my life. And why not? The most beautiful woman in half a dozen universes had just agreed to marry me, hadn't she? With Felira at my side, what did I have to be afraid of?

There was plenty of time to worry about later—well, *later*. Life is too short to fret yourself about something you have no control over. Whatever the identity of the man Hral Ssaroth held in such awe, he wasn't me. True, he might become me someday; but he wasn't me—nor I, he—yet.

Who knows what the future will bring?

When you get right down to it, who in his right mind would ever want to?

Felira was all the future I wanted or needed for the next couple of years. After the wedding, I would show her Europo-American. Maybe we would stop by and see Hal Benson, my old landlord. I smiled as I thought of "Crazy Hal" for the first time in nearly five years. I had once kidded him about his weird ideas—UFOs, aliens, civilizations beyond the stars. What kind of person would believe in such guff?

What kind of person would believe in Paratime, for that matter?

I wondered what Hal would do if I told him the truth about the events that had flowed from that night long ago when the UFO Spotters had used our rooming house for their meeting? He would probably get red in the face and accuse me of making fun of him. Then again, with Hal Benson, you could never be too sure.

Maybe the village idiot saving to buy his own cannon isn't so stupid after all. Maybe he sees a truth that the rest of us don't.

After Europo-American would come all the sights of the Confederation and the rest of Paratime. And someday soon, there would be the enigmatic Civilization X—where two-legged, armor-plated dinosaurs with cranial bulges and fully articulated hands might—or might not—rule. Dal's timetable had the first reconnaissance in force almost exactly one year from the day our rescuers had burst from the Syllsin Lunar portal. Dal had already hinted at a place for me on that expedition if I wanted it—as his "rabbit's foot," no doubt.

I figured a year was just about right for a honeymoon, and planned to take him up on his offer. Who knows, I might surprise him and actually do something useful.

For if one thing is as clear as the nose on Dal's face, it's that the inhabitants of Civilization X are too dangerous to be our enemies. Alien or human, man or beast, they will have to be won over as friends if Talador is not to find itself embroiled in another thousand-year war.

Luckily, the Taladorans are much more capable of making friends than they were even a few years ago. If the continuing crises that had beset them of late—Europo-American with its space program, Syllsin with its teleportation generator—have taught them anything, it is to be a bit more tolerant of people with ways other than their own.

I judge that lesson to be more important even than the discovery of the macrocluster structure of Paratime.

Of course, nothing ever happens in the course of human affairs without leaving a few rough edges to be worked on. Earlier I noted a tendency of some in the Ruling Council to ride roughshod over other cultures; but now at least, they were trying. It will be my job in the years ahead to keep nudging them in the right direction.

And if civilized relations can be established with an alien species, why not with the strain of humanity that rules the Dalgiri Empire? Nowhere is it written that Neanderthaler and Cro-Magnon must forever be locked in mortal combat. The example of the Aazmoran timeline is proof of that.

Which brings my thoughts to the subject of my "destiny" once more.

Maybe it is fated that I will one day help bring about an end to the Great Paratime War. At least it is nice to think about. One of my prime concerns since joining the

Time Watch has been to protect Europo-American from the depredations—unintentional or otherwise—of both sides. What better way to protect those I left behind than by ending the war altogether?

One thing's for sure. Whatever lies ahead, my life isn't going to be dull.

And after Civilization X, what then? The possibilities are as endless as the number of alternate universes across Paratime and the number of stars overhead. Those are the greatest infinities of all. And why not? Somewhere out there among the endless possibilities that are Paratime, there must be people who have traveled to the stars.

All we have to do is find them.

After Civilization X, maybe we will!